D0830306

# WAIT FOR DARK

## KIERSTEN MODGLIN

KIERSTEN
MODGLIN

WAIT FOR DARK is a work of fiction. Names, characters, places, images, and incidents are products of the author's imagination or are used fictitiously and are not to be construed as real. Any resemblance to actual events, locales, organizations, or persons—living or dead—is entirely coincidental and not intended by the author. The scanning, uploading, and distribution of this book without permission is a theft of the author's intellectual property. No part of this publication may be used, shared, or reproduced in any manner whatsoever without written permission except in the case of brief quotations embedded in critical articles and reviews. If you would like permission to use material from the book for any use other than in a review, please visit: kierstenmodglinauthor.com/contact

Thank you for your support of the author's rights.

Cover Design by Kiersten Modglin
Copy Editing by Three Owls Editing
Proofreading by My Brother's Editor
Formatting by Kiersten Modglin
Copyright © 2023 by Kiersten Modglin.
All rights reserved.

First Print and Electronic Edition: 2023
kierstenmodglinauthor.com

*This one's to the futures we dream of, the pasts we try to forget, the found families, and the hard truths we learn to share. This one's to you if life looks a little different than you thought it would.*

"...she always had the feeling that it was very, very dangerous to live even one day."

VIRGINIA WOOLF, *MRS. DALLOWAY*

# CHAPTER ONE

## HUDSON

I see it happen out of the corner of my eye.

A single hand gesture, but I register the move in seconds.

He thinks he's slick. Thinks he's really made something happen here.

He's probably done it hundreds of times. Probably gotten away with it.

She's just another woman to him. A conquest. Across the table in front of me, Constance is telling me about something that happened today. A client who did something... Or maybe something happened to a client.

Which client?

I don't know.

I can't listen. Can't focus. All I can do is watch as the woman reaches for her drink again while the man watches eagerly. She has no idea what's about to happen. Looking around the room, it seems no one else does either.

Just this prick and me.

"Sorry, would you excuse me for just a second?" I hold up a finger, cutting Constance off midsentence and scooting back from the table.

If she's angry, she doesn't let on. Instead, she flicks a bit of her blonde hair over her shoulder and turns to follow my gaze.

"Is everything alright?"

I don't answer. Can't. I'm up out of my seat and across the restaurant in a flash. I bump into the man on purpose, reaching to steal the drink from the woman's hand before it touches her lips.

*Woman* may not be an accurate term, I realize. She appears even younger up close—barely more than a girl. She's twenty-two, twenty-three, maybe. Can't be much older than that.

Her chestnut-brown eyes are wide as she stares at me, trying to understand what's happening. Waiting for whatever bad thing is about to happen to her.

She thinks I'm going to hurt her.

No, maybe she thinks I'm going to hit on her.

Wrong on either account.

"Hey, mate. What are you—"

"Trust me, you don't want to drink that," I say, ignoring the man behind me completely. Then thinking better of it, I turn to glance at him over my shoulder. "And I'm not your *mate*."

The bartender notices the commotion and approaches us with a wary look. "Everything okay?"

I hand him the cocktail glass, red liquid sloshing out onto my skin. "No. Everything's not okay. This man"—I jut my head toward the guy next to me, whose pale complexion suddenly seems almost translucent—"just slipped something into this young woman's drink. You should probably call the police."

"I... *What?*" the man shouts, backing away. "What the hell are you talking about? I didn't slip anything anywhere."

The woman's hands go to cover her lips, staring between us in horror. "Are you serious right now? You tried to drug me?" She already has her phone out, though whether she's calling 911 or texting her BFF, I can't be sure.

His jaw drops open with indignation. "You've got it all wrong!" He points at me. "He's lying."

I narrow my eyes at him. *And the Oscar goes to...* "I'm not. But feel free to stick around and explain your side of things to the cops."

"Bro, screw this. You don't know what you're talking about. Clearly, you need your eyes checked. I *moved* her drink. That's it."

"Ah, right, well, if that's the case, better save that drink." I hold out a hand, stopping the bartender from pouring it out. "The police may want to test it." I glance at the man again. "You know, in case I'm wrong."

Both hands up in angry defeat, the guy backs farther away from us and makes a beeline for the door without another word.

I ignore him as the bartender gives me a look of concern, then, at once, we direct our attention to the woman.

"Are you okay?" I ask.

She nods slowly, more out of habit than truly answering. "I... I think so." She eyes the cocktail. "I didn't drink anything."

It seems like more of a question than a statement, so I confirm, "No, he'd just slipped it in when you were looking at your phone. Did you know that man? Was he your date?" The bartender is still holding the contaminated drink in one hand.

"No, he was... He just approached me. He seemed nice enough. Normal." Her brown eyes are flecked with gold. Or maybe that's just the reflection of the lights overhead. Either way, they brim with tears as she speaks. "I didn't know him. I didn't think he'd try to... I mean, you always hear about it, but you never think..." She seems to shake the thought away. "I can't thank you enough."

"No need to thank me. I'm just glad you're okay. Try to be more careful with your drinks, okay? Keep them in your sight."

She reaches out, brushing a hand across my arm. "Of course. I feel so dumb. I know this stuff, I just... It's been a weird day, and I let my guard down. I know better." Again, she shakes her head, more tears forming in her eyes. "I'm sorry, what was your name? I don't think I asked. Can I buy you a drink? It's the least I can do..." She still seems out of it, reacting more out of politeness than anything else.

"No, that's okay. Just...just get home safely, okay?" Before I turn away, I add, "There are these ponytail holders they sell online now that unzip and fit on your cup to cover the top of your drink. You should get some. My wife never goes out without them."

The statement seems to bring her back down to earth. "Right. Thank you," she repeats, backing away from the bar. "I will. I'll look into those."

I feel strange letting her leave when she seems so shaken. Then again, it would be strange if she wasn't. "Is there anyone I can call for you? Are you going to be okay?"

"No. Yeah." She brushes off the question. "I'll be fine. I'm just startled, that's all. And embarrassed. I swear I'm usually so careful. I don't even remember taking my eyes off the drink. I guess I must've..." Her forehead wrinkles as her voice becomes soft. Powerless. "I feel so stupid."

"Don't. You're not. He was smart," I say. "They usually are. He waited for you to be distracted by something." I tap the phone in her hand. "It only took a second." Eyeing the bartender, I pat the counter. "You need to keep a better watch up here. Creeps like that are everywhere."

"Yeah, I will." He nods at me affirmatively, and though his words carry no bitterness, I expect it would probably be warranted if they did.

The kid is young, too. Barely old enough to be consuming the drinks he's tending, let alone to be in charge of the entire restaurant's well-being. But he'll never forget this, I can tell. Maybe it's his first time, but

I doubt it. And it won't be his last. I see it way too often.

"I should get back to my date," I say, pointing to the table where she's still waiting. "Just take care of yourself, okay? Can you get someone to walk her out when she's ready to leave? In case he's waiting outside."

Obviously shocked by the suggestion, her eyes widen. "I hadn't even thought of that. Thanks."

A bright-red blush covers her cheeks as the bartender tells her to come find him before she leaves, and with everything handled, I take my cue to walk away.

When I return to the table, Constance is watching me closely. "What was that all about? Do you know that woman?"

"No. Some asshole tried to spike her drink."

"And you stopped him?" Her eyes light up with approval.

"I don't think anyone else saw. I didn't have a choice." I'm trying to seem more modest than I feel, though I'm not sure it's working. In all actuality, I'm running on a cocktail of adrenaline coursing through my veins.

She reaches across the table, her fingers lacing with mine, and lowers her voice. "That was amazing. You might've just saved her life."

I shrug one shoulder. "And here I was, worried you'd be mad at me for interrupting our date night."

A smile decorates her face. "Of course not. I'm just glad you saw it happen before it was too late. That poor girl..." She glances over her shoulder toward the bar.

"Me too." I can't stand men who think they're entitled to everything, including women's bodies. They make the rest of us look bad.

"Girls can never be too careful nowadays. It's not like it used to be." Nostalgia weighs heavily on her words, and when she sighs again, I half expect her to want to end the night early and head home, so it catches me off guard when she instead says, "Do you... Are you ready to get out of here?"

———

Back at the hotel she's booked us for the night, our clothes are coming off before we've managed to shut the door all the way.

She has a fondness for my hero complex, apparently. I'd never noticed.

She eases herself out of the red chiffon gown slowly, never breaking eye contact. I've removed my tie but nothing else. I know better.

After our many years together, I know exactly what she wants.

Her dress hits the floor, revealing a set of lacy lingerie that must be new, and she steps toward me. She takes her time with each of my buttons, kissing her way down my chest.

Once my shirt is off, she removes my belt, making faster work of removing the bottom half of my clothing until I'm completely naked in front of her.

Her eyes trail the length of my body appreciatively. Hungrily. I never get tired of the way she looks at me.

Like I'm a work of art.

A statue meant to be adored by the masses, yet kept only for her.

She pulls me to the bed, where I'm finally encouraged to undress her the rest of the way.

"God, you're beautiful," I whisper. She likes compliments in bed. Needs them, maybe.

Nothing too dirty. Always classy.

I keep a mental checklist of everything she expects from me: every place I should touch, everything I should say and do, and when.

It's important for this to be everything she could dream of. Most men don't put enough thought into these things, but it's of the utmost importance.

She lies down, giving me firm directions about where she wants me, when she needs more pressure here or there, when I should move faster or slower, what to kiss, where to bite. She likes to be in command here, and I'm happy to oblige.

We both know I know this by now. I know the places that make her tremble, the moves that send her over the edge, but this is her game and I'm just a player.

She digs her nails into my back as I ease myself on top of her, locking eyes. As I slide inside her, all walls come down and she cries out, eyes closed. It's as if her entire body relaxes with the sigh she exhales.

I draw out the act, faster, then slower, bending her

over in front of me as she likes, and we end with her on top. I don't finish until she says I can.

I wouldn't dare.

When it's over, when our breathing has slowed and she drops down next to me on the bed, she smiles at me with that sated smile that says I've done my job.

"God, I think you've gotten better since last time."

I chuckle. "Lots of practice. And it helps that I have a good partner."

She runs a lazy hand over my chest, leaning over to kiss me gently before standing from the bed and getting dressed.

I gather my clothes from the floor and step into the bathroom. Seems silly, I guess. She's seen it all at this point, but I hate to ruin the illusion.

I clean myself up, rinse my mouth with the travel-sized bottle of mouthwash next to the sink, and get dressed. When I leave the room, she's already on the phone with someone from her work. She waves at me as I make my way past, looking as sharp as I did when I entered the restaurant three hours ago.

When I pull into the driveway a little over two hours later, I check my account and see that the deposit has made it in.

Three hours' work: An hour at dinner. Two hours at the hotel.

With any other client, I'd have Maddie request extra over the kiss on the mouth she slipped in at the end, but Constance has earned the extra just this once, so I let it slide.

I step out of the car and see the kitchen light flick on. Inside, I drop my keys into the designated bowl and hang my jacket on the rack.

"Hey, honey." Willa's voice comes from behind me and I turn around, smiling at my perfect wife. The sight of her still takes my breath away. "Long day?"

# CHAPTER TWO

## WILLA

People think being married to a gynecologist must be strange. If I had a nickel for every person who's ever questioned my sanity over letting my husband spend his days looking at other women's bits, I'd never have to work another day in my life.

Then again, most men I know couldn't identify a clitoris on a diagram and my husband can tell you about its more than ten thousand nerve endings over breakfast, so I've always thought of myself as the real winner.

Besides, even without all that, Hudson and I have been to hell and back, and somehow we made it out. I'm the luckiest woman in the world to be married to my best friend.

After telling me a bit about his day, he goes to take a shower and I plate the chicken and vegetables I've made.

I'm waiting at the table, sipping my glass of sauvignon blanc, when he appears. His skin is still red from the heat of the water. His preferred temperature is *melt your skin off your body*, which is why I refuse to take showers with him anymore. Though many nights during our early years ended in shower stalls much less nice than the one we have now.

He kisses my head before sitting down, and I run my fingers through his wet hair haphazardly, pulling his mouth to mine. The scent of his soap—spicy black pepper and cardamom—hits my nose, and I instantly relax. If I could find a candle that smells like him, I'd buy them up.

"This looks great," he says when we break apart.

"Thanks." I run a finger over my lips. "I tried that new marinade my mom sent over. Remember I told you about it? I used white wine instead of lemon juice, though."

He takes a small bite and gives a nod of approval. "How was your day?"

"Oh, it was fine. We met with a few new potential adoptive parents."

"Yeah? Got a good feeling about them?"

"I think so. There was one couple, in particular, I really liked. As soon as we have their home study approved, I have one specific birth mother in mind for them. I'd really like her to look over their file." I twist a strand of hair around my finger, thinking back over the meeting. "It seems like they could be a perfect fit. I just really hope it works out."

When I meet his eyes again, he's smiling at me as if I'm a child telling him about my future career as an astronaut. I know I'm over the top about my work sometimes, but I love what I do. Being a woman who plans on having no children of her own, most people think it's strange that I chose to go into adoption counseling as a career, but there's nothing better than seeing families seemingly created out of thin air and a lot of love.

Hudson got me the job. I'm up front about that. He's friends with a member of the board and pulled a few strings. It's nepotism, maybe, but then again, it's not like anyone was truly heartbroken over not getting chosen to make the measly wages I do. We do what we do out of love and passion, not for the money.

"Well, they're lucky to have your help," he says, taking another bite of his chicken. "Any other news?"

I think for a moment, running my fork over my food. "Oh, actually, yes." I sit up straighter, eyes wide, and from the look he's giving me, I must look like I'm losing my mind. Then again, that's exactly what it feels like. I take a deep breath to prepare myself. "Murphy wants you to be her doctor."

He'd been lifting another bite to his lips, but he stops and lowers it suddenly. "What?"

"Yes. She called me today."

"Wh-what? How?"

"Well, I'm no expert, but I'd say you could start with an ultrasound, maybe some bloodwork..." I start, teasing him.

He scowls at me playfully. "Alright, smart-ass. I know how to be a doctor. I meant, how would that work? I thought she already had a doctor."

"Well, she does, but I guess she doesn't really like him and wants to switch."

"And how is she?" He places his fork on his plate. "How far along? Did she say what her exact issues with her doctor are?"

I try to think, to calculate. "She's... I think she's three or four months along now. Due in September. So, not too far to switch, right?"

He tilts his head forward slightly, the weight of the request obvious. "Well, no. She can switch at any time. Who's she seeing now? What's wrong with him?" He dances around the refusal I sense is coming.

"She didn't really say, but she did mention he's not really listening to her. She's had morning sickness quite a bit, but he's not offered her anything to help. I think he's just been pretty dismissive of her in general." I pause, waiting for him to say more. When he doesn't, I prompt, "Well? What do you say? She wanted me to ask before she just called in and made the appointment."

"I don't know," he says softly. "Is that something you're comfortable with? Obviously, we want to get her to see a better doctor. We could get her in with someone else at the practice. Jake isn't taking on new patients, but I could get her on Tom's schedule, maybe. Or Megan's."

"I know. I agree it's a little strange. I wouldn't ask if I didn't think it was important to her. She's got no one, Hud. No family, no husband or boyfriend, just us. She trusts you." I reach out and pat his arm. "I wouldn't trust her to anyone else."

He sighs, and I have my answer even before he's given it verbally. "Alright. As long as you're both happy, I'm happy. Have her call my office and set it up."

"I will." I lift my phone from where it rests in front of my plate and text her to let her know he's agreed. Once the message is sent, I place it down and huff out a breath. "Can you believe she's going to be a mom? I still don't think it's totally set in for me. I mean, *a mom*. How unreal is that?"

He shoves another bite of food in his mouth, chewing thoughtfully. "So, you think she'll keep it, then?"

"She hasn't said for sure," I admit, running a finger across the rim of my wineglass. "But it seems like it. I mean, she's still sort of freaking out, but she's been talking long term. Potentially moving out of her place into something with more space. It sounds like she's going to try."

"Good for her." He takes a sip of his wine, swishing it in his mouth. "It'll be good for her. Settle her down some. You know I never liked the idea of her going out so late on her own." Something dark crosses his face.

"What is it?"

"Nothing."

"You made a face."

He takes another bite. "It's nothing, really. Just... There was a girl at the restaurant earlier. Someone slipped something into her drink." He shakes his head, massaging the space above his eyebrow.

The sentence takes my breath away. "Oh no... That's awful. What happened? Did he get caught? Is she okay?"

"Yeah. I stopped him before anything happened."

I tilt my head toward my shoulder. "*You* stopped him?"

He nods, pinching his bottom lip between his thumb

and forefinger. "Yeah. No one else saw him do it. I didn't want to get involved, but I didn't have a choice."

"Well, thank god you noticed him. That poor girl. Sometimes, I really hate men. No offense."

"None taken." He smirks with his mouth full of food. "We *are* kind of the worst."

"That's why I bought those cup covers for Murphy."

"And for you," he pipes up.

"And for me," I agree. "Though I can't remember the last time I had use for them. I'm an old, married lady now." I wiggle my fingers at him, showing off my ring.

He laughs, lifting my hand farther from the table and pressing it to his lips. "Married, yes, but far from old."

I swallow. "Speaking of *old*, how did... How did the rest of your night go?"

"Fine." His expression goes serious, and he withdraws his hand. "According to plan."

"Everything went smoothly?"

"Yep. Money's already in the account."

"Good." I smile, checking my phone when I see a reply from Murphy come in confirming that she'll call tomorrow to set an appointment.

His hand slides over to grasp mine, his expression stoic. "I love you."

He always tells me this a few extra times on nights after he's been with a client. Maybe he thinks I need to hear it. Maybe he just needs to say it.

"I love you more," I vow.

"Not possible." He leans back in his chair, worry etching a line across his forehead. He's nearly cleared his plate while most of my food sits untouched. It usually takes a few hours for the knots of fear to unwind themselves for me, making space for nourishment again.

My husband, on the other hand, has obviously worked up quite an appetite.

I can only imagine the responses I'll get when people find out Hudson is going to be delivering my best friend's baby.

But, then again, it's far from the most scandalous part of our marriage, wouldn't you say?

# CHAPTER THREE

## HUDSON

It started in college.

You're probably wondering, right? I should just go ahead and clear the air and say it was never the plan.

Then again, going to medical school in the first place was never really the plan.

Not that I didn't *want* to go. It was all I wanted. During my fourth grade Parents Day, one little girl's father, a surgeon, came to talk to us. He was dressed just like I'd seen in movies: white coat, scrubs.

He let us listen to our heartbeats with his stethoscope and passed around tongue depressors for us to take home. Most of the kids used them to whack each other in the back of the head until our teacher collected them, but I held on to mine.

There was something so cool about it, even back then. The idea of saving people. Of fixing things. The idea that every day, I could do the impossible and have all the answers.

It was intoxicating.

But I was just a little boy with two dead parents, who was on his sixth set of foster parents in the last two years. I didn't exactly have a path to medical school laid out in front of me.

No one was on pins and needles, ready to show me the way.

But I worked hard. Even back then, I wanted to impress people. Defy the odds. There was something addictive about earning the approval of others.

A therapist might say I had an unhealthy obsession with being a good boy. I didn't miss the shock on my teachers' faces when I turned in assignments on time or their pride when I passed the assignments by more than a hair.

When I graduated, I wasn't exactly at the top of my class, but I wasn't at the bottom either. I "had potential," my guidance counselor said, even when she looked reluctant to speak the words. If I was somewhere stable, with a quiet place to study and food in my stomach every night, she seemed to think there was a path where I could get what I wanted after all.

I received a few scholarships and grants that partially covered my first few years of school, but it wasn't enough. Hell, it wasn't even close to being enough.

I worked in a bar at night, putting up with rowdy classmates and sleazy men trying to pick up the local college kids, and tucked away every cent that didn't go to housing, food, or gas for my old beat-up truck. I was used to going without, but my long hours and late

nights meant I still didn't have time to study like I needed to.

I was falling behind.

Failing.

For the first time in my life, even my best suddenly wasn't good enough.

My choices, as far as I could see them, were to either pick up every extra shift I had in order to keep the studio apartment I shared with two other students or skip the extra shifts in favor of studying, but doing that would literally mean losing the roof over my head.

I was already at the bottom. There was nowhere left to downgrade, no cheaper options, but I was stubborn.

I wouldn't give up until I had no other choice.

And, as luck would have it, when I needed it most, the universe handed me one.

It was late in the year, close to Christmas, though that meant nothing to me as I had no one to return home to. Instead, I picked up all the extra shifts at the bar available to me and reveled in the time without classwork piling up.

I was behind the bar one night when a young woman caught my eye. *Catherine.* I recognized her from one of my classes, though it would've been easy not to realize it was her. The usually plain girl I'd sat next to a dozen times had transformed into something different there in the dimly lit room. She was dressed up, for one thing, wearing makeup I'd never seen her wear, but there was a confidence to her I hadn't noticed before.

Maybe I was just lonely since most of the campus had gone home for the holiday break. Maybe it was fate.

Either way, I carried a drink over to her table and introduced myself. To my surprise, she knew who I was. When I asked if she had plans after my shift, she told me she was on a date.

At first, I thought she was blowing me off, but I took the hint and retreated back to my work. It didn't matter anyway. I had no time for a relationship, though I wouldn't have turned down a casual night of fun.

Within a few minutes, though, her *date* showed up. He was in his fifties, by my best guess, round in the tummy and balding.

Was she really blowing me off for him?

I mean, I didn't think I was the world's greatest catch, but come on.

The next night, she was back in a new dress with a new man. Over the holiday, I watched her come in over and over, each time with someone new. She seemed to be attracted exclusively to older men. Much older.

When I finally decided to ask her about it, I broached the subject carefully, making a joke about her taste in dates.

She seemed uneasy. "Why do you care?"

"I don't, I guess. I just think someone as pretty as you could do better."

She scoffed. "Gee, thanks. Is that supposed to be a line?"

"It's a compliment, actually. And hey, I'm not judging."

"Funny because it sounds like you are." She moved to stand, but I reached out and caught her arm. She swung around, her fist clipping my jaw. I released her, in equal measure, shocked and impressed.

"What the hell was that?" I rubbed my jaw. My head throbbed, both from embarrassment and frustration. Luckily, the bar was too crowded for anyone to have noticed.

"Don't ever touch me again."

My hands went up in surrender. "Yeah, okay. You got it. Sorry. I just..." I stepped back. "I'm sorry. I didn't want you to rush out. I'll leave you alone."

I turned around, prepared to leave, but she shouted after me.

"If you must know..."

I turned back, studying the apprehension in her eyes. "I come here because, *normally,* you make me feel safe."

I tapped a finger on my jaw. "Safe, hmm? You sure about that?"

She smiled and stepped closer. "I see you watching me from across the room. When I'm meeting someone new, it helps, knowing someone has my back."

Pride swelled in my chest. Even without knowing it, I'd done something right. I'd managed to be exactly what she needed. "Well, I'm glad I could be of service."

I started to turn away again but froze when she spoke.

"And, for the record, they aren't exactly my *type*. But beggars can't be choosers."

I turned around, lowering my brows and scrutinizing

her. My eyes trailed up her body unabashedly. "I hardly think you have to beg."

She rolled her eyes, glancing away. "It's for school, Hudson. I'm... I need help paying for school."

"What do you mean?" I asked the question, though I had a sinking feeling in my gut that told me I already knew the answer.

She stared at me, the corners of her eyes pinching together. "I think you know."

"You mean you're... You're sleeping with them for money?"

She was slow to nod, not meeting my gaze.

Maybe she expected me to tell her it was a terrible idea. Maybe she thought I'd beg her to stop. Then again, maybe she sensed the same desperation in me that she felt in herself.

I stepped closer, lowering my voice more. "Holy shit. Is it good money?"

She met my eyes finally, squaring her shoulders. "Good enough I have my own apartment and don't have to live on ramen. Good enough I haven't had to take out any student loans."

I swallowed, a world opening up for me in my mind. I wondered if she could sense it. Checking over my shoulder, I studied the bar. What if I never had to go back? Never had to take another extra shift?

"How?" I croaked.

"How?"

"I want in."

She smiled, sizing me up. "I'll talk to my manager."

23

She'd said *manager*, not madam or pimp like I'd expected her to. Was that only what they were called in the movies? Either way, I liked her term. It made it all feel less wrong. Like we were doing a job, just like anything else.

And a week later, when she returned to the bar, she slid me a business card with a phone number.

"You're in."

"Yeah?"

"Call Maddie, our manager. She'll get you set up."

Just like that, I was ready to combine two of my favorite things, sex and money, and change my entire life. Just like that, I could finally stop treading water and catch my breath.

This was all I'd been waiting for, and all I had to do was say yes.

No-brainer.

# CHAPTER FOUR

When I first met Hudson, I recognized him from around campus, but we'd never talked. That night, I finally worked up the courage to approach him with a little shove from my friends. It was on a Friday night at a bar near campus.

He was sitting alone at a table, drinking a beer. When I sat down, his eyes widened. It was as if he'd seen a ghost, so I had to wonder if he'd seen me around, too.

He was average height and was somewhere in between muscular and skinny. His dark-brown hair flipped out around his ears, and he had the sort of smile that made me want to lean in and listen to whatever he was saying. His green eyes had a blue ring around the irises and he stared at me from behind thick, long eyelashes.

He was conventionally handsome, but in a way that wasn't imposing. He didn't seem to think the sun rose and set with him, like some of the men I'd dated since starting college.

"Hey," I said when I realized he still hadn't greeted me. Instead, he was scrutinizing me as if I'd walked in with an Easter basket or dressed in a superhero costume. As if *I* was the strange one. Maybe he just wasn't used to women making the first move.

"Hey." He smiled, leaning forward. "I wasn't expecting you. Normally they're..." He cut himself off.

I wasn't sure whether to be offended or confused. I settled on both. "I'm sorry?"

"No, it's just... Wow. You're a nice surprise."

Heat crept up my neck, and I ran a hand through my hair. It was darker blonde than usual since I'd been skipping my highlights in favor of things like food and college textbooks. Once I'd graduated high school, my mom made it clear I was on my own. Not that she'd ever been much help to begin with. "Well, thank you. I'm Willa."

"Henry," he said, holding out a hand.

"Nice to meet you, Henry."

"Do you want a drink, or would you rather go someplace quieter?"

His forwardness shocked me. "Um, I'll get a drink. Be right back." No way in hell was I going to allow him to bring me a drink. I'd been to all the campus safety seminars. I knew better than that.

When I returned with a beer of my own a few minutes later, his was almost gone. There was a new flush to his cheeks. He slid closer to me, resting a hand on my thigh.

As surprising as it was, I had to admit, his confidence was a major turn-on. Where had he been hiding this guy on campus? Every time I saw him, he was shy and quiet. This was like a new persona.

"So, you're the *wine and dine* type, hmm?" he whispered, studying me as if I were a puzzle he was trying to solve.

I chuckled. "As opposed to what? The *jump straight into bed with you* type?"

He grinned. "Hey, it's totally up to you. I'm at your service tonight."

"I'm a proper lady, Henry. You'll do well to remember that," I teased him.

"Yes, ma'am." His eyes sparkled in the dim bar. He smelled of something spicy and metallic. Pepper, maybe? Whatever it was, it had me leaning in for more.

"So, what are you going to school for?"

He swallowed. His hand froze in place on my thigh before he lifted it and leaned back, as if the conversation had caught him off guard. "Um, I'm still deciding. Are... Are you in school, too?"

So, he didn't recognize me. My ego only suffered a minor blow, but I recovered quickly. "Yeah. I'm going to be a social worker."

Something darkened in his eyes, and he took another drink of his beer. "Saving the world one troubled kid at a time, hmm?"

"Yeah, something like that."

He looked skeptical but merely said, "Hmm."

"What? You don't think I can?"

"I think you can do whatever you want." The charm was back, the casual smile, the confidence.

"You can tell me the truth," I assured him. What was it about my personality and looks that made people underestimate me? I was capable of so much more than people gave me credit for.

He seemed to resist the urge for a moment but eventually said, "Well, it's got nothing to do with you. To be honest, I just think the system is flawed."

"I agree with you. Maybe that's why I want to help."

"Maybe you will."

"I will. And *when* I do, you'll think back over that one special night you had with the woman who changed the world." I waved my hand in the air dramatically, like a princess or pageant queen.

His smirk was back. Cocky and carefree. It filled my stomach with warmth. "Fair enough. Something tells me I won't forget it."

"We'd better make sure of it, hmm?" I took another sip of my beer, picking at the paper wrapped around the bottle. "So, are you from around here?"

"Where do you want me to be from?"

I stared at him. "What kind of question is that? Is this like *Build-A-Man* or something?"

"If you want it to be."

I laughed. "Seems like someone raised you right, Henry. Determined to make a woman happy. I like that."

He leaned in farther, his breath hot on my skin. "You have no idea how happy."

I snorted. He was really trying, I'd give him that. "Wait, was that a line?"

"Apparently not a very good one, if it didn't work."

"I'm not interested in hearing lines. Why don't you just try being real?"

His gaze faltered, and he stared at me like I was suggesting something ridiculous. As if no one in his life allowed him to be real, ever.

Was that the case?

I shot a glance at my friends across the room. Murphy, Shontelle, and Ashley were sitting at the round table, cackling over a joke I couldn't hear. At that moment, I was so thankful to have friends who knew the real me.

"What do you mean?" he asked eventually, drawing my attention back to him.

"Like... I mean, I don't know. For half a second, stop trying to do whatever it is you think you're supposed to be doing and just be yourself. I'm not expecting anything from you, Henry. I don't need to be charmed. I just want to get to know you."

"Really? Are... Are you sure?" I might as well have just handed that man a million dollars, the way he was staring at me. He scratched the hair at his temple, tucking a strand behind his ear.

"Well, unless *yourself* is a serial killer, yeah."

He laughed then, really laughed this time. A full-bodied laugh that I felt in my own belly. "Decidedly not a serial killer."

I shrugged. "That's what they all say."

I realized then how much I was enjoying talking to him, even if ninety percent of what he said was bullshit. He was easy to talk to, easier to listen to.

"Well, okay. If we're being real…" He cracked his knuckles, leaning back in his chair. "I'm going to be a doctor."

"A doctor? Really? Wow. That's actually impressive. Why wouldn't you want to tell me that?"

"Well…" He hesitated, obviously wrestling with what to admit next.

"Tell me."

His eyes locked with mine, and it was as if everyone else in the room disappeared. Everything happened in slow motion. Nothing else mattered. "It's just that I don't usually *do* this."

"Do what?"

"Talk," he said frankly.

I was quiet for a moment, trying to understand what he was saying. "You don't usually *talk*?"

"Not really. No."

"As in, at all? To your dates or friends or…"

"Either, or. I don't really have time for friends. I'm always working or studying. And most of my dates aren't interested in talking."

I drank in what he was saying, letting it wash over me. "Wow. Well, that's just sad."

His frown confirmed just how sad it was, as if he hadn't realized it until right then.

"Not really. It's just… It is what it is, you know? I mean, most of the women I see aren't that into talking."

He twirled the beer bottle in his fingers rhythmically, watching the light reflecting on the glass. Finally, he looked up at me with a sort of softness that took my breath away. "You're kind of a first, Willa."

I pressed my lips together, willing myself to come up with a response that didn't sound like I was melting into my chair over the lines I'd sworn not to want. I settled on saying, "I'm the first woman who's ever wanted to talk to you? Wow, you know how to make an impression, don't you?"

"I..." His head cocked to the side. "Well, what can I say? I make my impression in other ways."

I rolled my eyes with a dramatic sigh. "There you go again. Now I see why women prefer you to be silent."

He snorted. "Is that what you'd prefer?"

We were already comfortable together. That's what I remember most about that night. How utterly at ease he made me.

"I prefer you to be real."

"If I'm being real... I don't understand why you're here." Suddenly, it was as if he was stone-cold sober.

"What?"

"I mean, don't tell Maddie I said this, but you could get any guy you want. I hardly think you need help in this department. Are you a virgin or something? Wanting to get it out of the way?"

I bristled at his words, the blood draining from my face. "Excuse me?"

"I'm sorry." He put up a hand to stop me from getting up. "Normally, I wouldn't say anything. It's all supposed to be part of the fantasy, I know. But if you're asking me to be real, I have to say it. Why are you here right now?"

"I am...so lost." I pushed my drink away from me. What was I missing?

He leaned forward over the table. "I mean, there's no shame in it, but I'm just trying to figure out exactly what I'm supposed to be for you tonight. Maddie usually—"

"I'm sorry. Who's Maddie?"

"My manager..." His words came to a halt. "Oh god. I'm sorry. Do you know who I am?"

"Are you drunk right now? Of course I know who you are. You're Henry. You told me."

"Right." He drank the last of his beer, rapping his knuckles against the table as if he was suddenly uncomfortable. "I'm asking, were you supposed to meet me tonight?"

"Oh, shoot. Were you on a blind date or something?" I launched myself out of my chair, tugging at the hem of my shirt. Compared to most of the girls there, I was underdressed in jeans and a sweater. Of course he wasn't interested in me when he had so many other people to choose from. What the hell did I think was happening? "I'll just go."

He reached for my arm, stopping just shy of grasping it. "Wait. There's been a misunderstanding."

"Excuse me, are you Henry?"

A voice from behind me startled us both, and when I turned around, there was an older woman standing a few feet away. She moved forward. Her graying hair was pulled back from her face in an updo, and she was wearing heavy makeup and a sparkling black cocktail dress. She was staring right through me, hardly noticing I was there.

*This was his date?*

Apparently, I wasn't his type.

"Oh my god." I stepped back, preparing to walk away, but he caught my arm, his eyes locked on mine.

When he spoke, he never looked away from me, though he was addressing the woman. "Sorry, no. I'm not. I'm... I'm Hudson."

# CHAPTER FIVE

## HUDSON

At first, Willa and I were just friends. She never judged me for what I did, which was refreshing, considering I'd never been brave enough to talk to anyone other than the people I worked with about my profession.

Still, I couldn't help falling in love with her. Maybe I fell for her that very first night. It was the only reason I could come up with for revealing my true first name in front of a client.

Maddie had been clear. We had to have a cover story. A new name. We were nobody and everybody all at once. Malleable. We were to be whatever our client wanted. Dress how they asked. Meet where they preferred. It was all a fantasy and we were the faceless, and sometimes nameless, actors filling a role.

Most of my clients were wealthy, older women. Widows. Bored housewives. Business people who had no time for relationships.

I was just a warm body to them. It was transactional.

That's how I explained it to Willa. How I made her understand that, in a way, it was just like any other job.

Maddie took care of the website, scheduled the jobs, booked the hotels, and accepted the payments from clients. She waited for my text to let her know I'd arrived safely, and I waited for hers to let me know she'd received the payment. We both held our breath a little bit until I texted her to let her know I was leaving in one piece, and she lined up my appointments to get tested weekly.

It was a job and I was a pawn, albeit a well-paid pawn. Truth be told, I didn't hate it. I was too young to worry about feeling objectified or care too much about my safety.

For the first time in my life, I didn't have to worry about where my next meal was coming from. Besides, fearing for my life wasn't exactly new to me.

I'd take my chances with the widows who wanted to gag me or walk on my back with stilettos and the house-wives who wanted to see me bleed.

I was just a toy in a bed.

A doll.

Something to play with when they were bored.

A way to pass an hour.

Fulfill a fantasy.

I had no time for relationships anyway.

At least, I didn't until I met Willa. Once she was in my life, all I could think of was finding a way to make it all okay in her eyes. To make myself worthy of her.

When I graduated medical school—the day I told Maddie I was quitting—with zero student loan debt and an entire future I wasn't meant to have in front of me, I proposed to her. We'd never gone on an official date. I'd never kissed her, let alone anything else, but I knew, in my heart, I'd just been waiting for her.

Luckily, she'd been waiting for me too.

---

Of course, as much as our love story has been somewhat of a fairy tale, life isn't a fairy tale and I have the scars to prove it. As a medical resident, I made not much more than my new wife was making as an entry-level social worker for the county, which was practically nothing. While I had no student loan debt, she had plenty. We struggled to keep up, never mind ever getting ahead.

Between the credit card debt we both had, the car payments we had to take out to get to our new jobs, and the everyday bills it takes to survive, during a particularly bad month or when an unexpected expense arose, it was easy to slip back into old habits, though never without talking with her first.

I want to reiterate: *it is a transaction.*

I'm not cheating on her. I would never. We've both agreed. I'd sooner die than do anything to jeopardize my marriage. I'm performing a job just like we both do during the day.

And now, with things having settled down for us financially, with fewer emergencies and bad months popping up, the jobs I take are very rare, highly paid, and only for clients I've worked with in the past.

It's just a way to pay off the rest of our debt and build up a savings account. A way to someday afford a nicer house without saddling ourselves with a mountain of debt and stress to do it.

Willa and I grew up in financially unstable homes, to varying degrees, and the thought of ever falling into the paths laid out by our parents terrifies us. I refuse to ever live like that again—wondering where my next meal will come from, choosing whether to pay the mortgage or the electric bill. In the back of my mind, the ugly truth is always right there: when you have no money to fall back on, no family to help, we're all just a few bad months away from losing it all.

If there's any way I can prevent that fear from creeping in, prevent it from causing my wife an ounce of worry, I'll do it.

Without question.

Every time.

It's not a forever plan, maybe it's not even a good plan, but for now, it's saved our lives and our futures more times than I can count. Besides, like I said, I'm always happy to be of service.

# CHAPTER SIX

## WILLA

The door to the restaurant swings open, the gust of wind from outside sending a warm rush of air through the building.

Spring is finally settling in, bringing with it a sense of peace. I'm a fan of spring only because it means summer is on its heels. Mostly, spring feels like a taste of what's to come.

I wave at her from across the room, and when her eyes land on me, she waves back and heads my way. As usual, she appears frazzled. Her hair is pulled back in a messy ponytail, and her jacket is unzipped and slips off her shoulder when she removes her purse and hangs it on the back of her chair. She leans down, and I wrap my best friend in a hug from my seat.

"Sorry I'm late," she says, easing into her chair.

"Like I expected any less."

She tears the paper from the straw and tosses it at me

before dropping the straw into the lemonade I ordered for her. "Hey, it's not my fault traffic is a nightmare."

"Fair enough." I don't point out that this restaurant is ten minutes closer to her apartment than my house and I still managed to arrive thirty minutes before her. When making plans with Murphy, I always bring a book and clear my schedule for a few hours. She runs on her own clock, I swear. "So, how are you feeling?"

"Why does everyone keep asking me that?" She scowls, looking away. She isn't angry with me, just scared of the question. I'm still not entirely sure she knows this is really happening.

"Maybe because they want to know."

"I'm fine, Wills," she says, using the nickname she stuck me with when we shared a homeroom class in fifth grade. We've been attached at the hip ever since. "Honest."

"Any more morning sickness?"

"Oh god. More like *all* the morning sickness. And afternoon sickness. And midnight sickness. Whoever named that shit should be sued."

I grin apologetically. I can't relate or pretend to know how she feels, but I want to be there for her however I can. I reach into my purse and pull out a bag of ginger candies I ordered online. "I didn't realize it was so bad until you told me. I read that these can help. I thought you could keep them in your pocket when you're at work."

She eyes the bag, then tears it open, untwists the

cellophane wrapping from the candy, and pops it into her mouth. "Thanks. Seriously, I'll try anything."

"Hudson should be able to prescribe you something to help, too. When are you seeing him?"

"Eh, in like two weeks," she says. "Not soon enough." Her hand moves to her stomach absentmindedly, though there's still very little evidence of her condition.

"Was that the earliest appointment? Surely he could get you in sooner."

"No." She puts a hand up. "Trust me, I appreciate it, but I don't want any special favors. I already feel weird enough about using your husband as my doctor."

"But you're the one who suggested it."

"Yeah, because I trust you guys. I trust him. That doesn't mean it isn't completely freaking me out that he's about to be all up in my business." She waves a hand in the general direction of said business.

"It's what he does. Trust me, he's not thinking anything about it. Vaginas are like necks to him. You wouldn't feel weird about him looking at your neck, would you?"

She turns her attention to her napkin, rolling the edge between her fingers. "I think I'd feel weird if anyone started examining my neck, to be honest."

The eye roll I give her is totally warranted. "Well, look, Hudson already said he can get you on the schedule of someone else in his office if you'd prefer that. We just want whatever will make you most comfortable. That's what matters."

"I know. I appreciate it." She's serious for half a

second. "Just don't get mad at me if your husband takes one look at what I'm working with and falls madly in love with me and we have to run away together."

"Yeah, well, I'll take my chances. Just don't run too fast. It's not good for the baby." My words are meant to be a joke, but they have a sobering effect.

She places her hands in her lap. "Wills, am I really doing this? Am I having a baby?"

"You're having a baby," I confirm.

She looks down, her voice cracking as she does everything possible to avoid eye contact. "What if I'm no good at it?"

My answer requires no hesitation. It's one I've spent the past few weeks rehearsing. "You will be. We'll make sure you are." I reach for her hand. "Everything's going to be okay. I promise you."

I just wish I was as sure as I sound.

# CHAPTER SEVEN

## HUDSON

Maddie only calls after dark.

That's the arrangement. My attempt at keeping my day job, and the rest of my life, separate from this.

That is why, when I step out of a patient's room and into the hallway of the practice, I'm surprised to see her number on my screen.

I have it memorized after all these years, but never saved. That would be against her rules.

I consider not answering it. She's breaking one of *my* rules, after all, but for her to call in the middle of the day has me worried something's wrong.

I jog down the hall and step into my office, turning the "In Meeting" sign around to prevent the nurses from disturbing me before closing the door.

With a deep breath, I press the phone to my ear. "Hello?"

"Henry." Her voice is slow and raspy, as it's always been. We've never met in person, but I picture her sitting around a luxury apartment, smoking cigarettes every time we speak. I have no idea if that's accurate. "I have a new client for you."

We don't bother with niceties or greetings. Never have. This business isn't a friendly one.

"A new client?" I keep my voice low. "No. You know I only take already established clients. We've discussed this." Multiple times, actually, though I don't throw in that last part.

"Yes, I know. But this one requested you personally. She was referred by a friend."

I don't take this personally. It's the nature of our business. We aren't people to them. There's no sentimental value or jealousy about our relationships, if you want to call them that, though I'd prefer you didn't. We're objects. And, when we're particularly good at what they use us for, which I happen to be, sometimes they pass us along to their friends like good little toys. It's all par for the course.

"What friend?"

"Constance."

That one name is all I need to hear. Constance is the client I care about most—the only one I trust. She's been with me since college. A once- or twice-a-year booking that I can rely on. We know each other well enough now that we're a well-oiled machine.

Maybe that's a bad analogy.

"I was just with her. She didn't mention a referral."

Maddie doesn't have to tell me she wouldn't. That it would interrupt the fantasy. For the evening, we're just a pair of mad-for-each-other lovers. Why would she break the spell by mentioning someone else? By mentioning our arrangement at all?

Most clients wouldn't, but somehow I expected more from Constance.

It's my own fault. I should know better.

"I don't know." Maddie doesn't know about Willa. She doesn't know anything about my personal life. It's better that way. So I can't tell her I haven't discussed taking on new clients with my wife. "I'm busy, and we've talked about me not taking on new clients—"

"She's offered three times your usual rate. Says she only needs two hours. No unusual requests. I've already checked her out. It's straightforward. Easy money."

Easy for her to say.

I swallow.

"When?"

"Tonight. Nine o'clock. No dinner. Straight to the hotel. I'll send you the details."

# CHAPTER EIGHT

## WILLA

When I hear Hudson's car pull into the driveway, I've just walked in the door myself. My back hurts and my feet are throbbing from being on them all day planning our annual spring fundraiser.

I open the door and step back out on our small stoop, grinning at him. Despite being married for nearly five years, the butterflies I get in my stomach when I see him have never waned. I think it's because we were friends for so long before we officially became a couple. Before he finally admitted he felt the same way I did.

Because the truth is, I think I fell for him the first night we met. There's something so real and honest about Hudson that draws you to him. I still find him completely irresistible.

"Hey, honey," he says, jogging the final stretch to reach me. He's dressed in his navy scrubs, though his white coat has been left at the office. "Missed you."

"Missed *you*. How was traffic?"

"Not bad, actually. For you?"

"I took sixty-five home, so it was fine."

He brushes a bit of hair from my face. "You guys are planning the fundraiser, right?"

I nod, setting my purse down on the sofa table near the door and pulling off my jacket.

"Anything I can do to help? I've already talked to Jake about upping our sponsorship for the year. We're good to go."

"Awesome, thanks."

He drops his keys into the bowl next to my purse. "What were you thinking for dinner?"

"I don't know. How about we order in? You look about as exhausted as I feel."

He chuckles. "Is that your way of telling me I look bad?"

"You never look bad." I pat his chest. "I like you sleepy."

"Why's that?" He looks genuinely confused.

"Because I'm the only one who gets that version of you."

He pauses for half a second, then leans down and presses his lips to mine. "Always will be."

I grin. "So, is that a yes to takeout?"

"Sounds good. Want me to order?"

"Sure. Whatever sounds good to you." He follows me to the bedroom, where we both strip out of our clothes and change into pajamas.

Once he's dressed, he sinks onto the bed with a sigh. "Listen, I need to talk to you about something."

"Uh-oh. That sounds ominous." I turn to the mirror, pulling my hair up while watching his reflection.

"Maddie called earlier."

I freeze and spin around. I've never met Maddie. In fact, I assume Maddie is a fake name like she requires Hudson to use when he's working. But she feels like a permanent fixture in my marriage. At times, our saving grace. At others, a weeping sore we must manage.

"And?"

"She wants me to meet with a new client."

I press my lips together. Inhale. "But you aren't taking on new clients."

That has been the deal. As annoying as it is to even let him see older clients, I know he's doing what it takes to get us out of debt, to set us up for the life we both desperately want.

The life neither of us had before.

I know he's doing it for us—that I've had to ask him to do it for us in the past—so I have to be careful with my complaints now.

Still, at least with his usual clients, the ones he's worked with for years, it's just a handful of times a year and there's less risk involved.

New clients bring with them a whole host of uncertainties.

"I know, but she's offered to pay three times my usual rate."

I sink down on the bed next to him. "I don't like the sound of that, Hud. Why would she offer that? What do we know about her?"

*Nothing* is the answer. Because we never know anything about his clients. Not their last names, not where they live or where they work, not why they choose him.

"She was referred to me by Constance."

I glance down at my lap, gathering my hands together. Sometimes I wonder how we got here.

"So, you want to do it?"

"Well, I don't *want* to, no, but three times my rate is a big deal. Just two hours and we could nearly pay off the rest of one of our cars. Or replace the fence in the back-yard before it falls in, if nothing else."

My eyes widen as I try to do the mental math. He's right, as usual. It's hard to turn it down when just a few hours could give us so much.

"And I trust Constance. She wouldn't send someone to me if she didn't know her well. I mean, it's not like these conversations come up organically between friends." He pauses. "I don't want to let her down, but if you think it's a bad idea, I won't do it. You know that. It's all up to you."

I pick at a piece of skin near my nail, weighing our options. "When would she need you?"

"Tonight." His Adam's apple bobs as he swallows. "At nine."

I'm used to the short notice of this situation and of our lives. Both of Hudson's jobs require him to cancel plans at the drop of a hat. The way I see it, they're not all that different.

It's the way I have to see it to keep myself sane.

"For how long?"

"Two hours. Just two hours."

I nod, then look over at him. "Fine. Tell her you'll do it."

"Are you sure?"

"No," I admit. "But I trust you. And if you think it's worth your time, I'm in."

He kisses my head. "Not much longer of this, you know? Once both of the cars and the house are paid off, I can walk away. We'll be debt-free."

It feels like a pipe dream, and yet, with every job he accepts, every extra payment we can make, I watch our balances getting smaller. It's happening. With any luck, both our cars will be paid off in just a few more years and the house will be a ten- or fifteen-year mortgage rather than thirty. Someday, it will have all been worth it. I have to believe that.

People think being married to a doctor means a life of lavish luxury, but I'm afraid it just isn't so. Hudson makes more money now that he's out of residency, but I make pennies in comparison, and with all of our monthly bills and debt, most months, we barely scrape by. There's rarely enough to put into savings for a rainy day.

*This* is our rainy-day fund.

Our future.

Growing up with parents who fought every day of my life over money, wearing clothes that were outdated or too small, never having birthday parties or going on vacations, never having enough of anything to fit in with the kids I so desperately wanted to, I understood from an early age just how powerful money is.

Hudson had it worse, I know. My parents took me to food banks when things got bad; his just let him starve.

Still, we're on the same page about these things. We have to pay off our debt. We need to have savings that will help us survive if anything goes wrong.

Struggling is not an option when we have such an easy way out.

I just have to trust that this won't last forever. That there's a light at the end of this tunnel.

I just have to trust him.

# CHAPTER NINE

## HUDSON

Maddie prefers to use the same hotel for all of our appointments if we can help it. She's worked out a deal with most of the staff, so there are no questions asked about our frequent coming and going, no pun intended, and they look out for us should things go awry. I've been around to witness them calling an ambulance when an appointment goes wrong.

I walk past the front desk, stopping long enough to get my key card, though the room payment has already been taken care of by Maddie, and they don't ask to see my ID. Then I make my way to the elevator, looking as fresh as if I'd just walked off a red carpet. My hair is just washed and slicked back, and the suit I'm wearing is more expensive than anything else hanging in my closet. It's an old favorite, and when clients don't request that I wear anything specific, it's become my reliable default.

Everyone loves a man in a suit, right?

I study my reflection in the metal doors. You'd never know how exhausted I feel just by looking at me. I'm good at my job, which means I know how to look fresh-faced, even coming off a ten-hour shift. I know how to groom myself head to toe, *manscape* as Willa calls it, how to shape my facial hair, which creams to use on my skin, and I can do it all in under an hour when pressed for time.

It's old hat for me now.

Just like that, I'm someone new and no one at all.

I'm whatever she wants, this mysterious new client.

As I step off the elevator, I type out a text to Maddie, letting her know I've arrived.

I never know whether I'll make it to the room before my clients, so as I turn down the hallway on the eighth floor and approach the door, I freeze when I hear a sound that turns my blood cold.

"*Stop! Stop it! Please!*" A woman's desperate cries can barely be heard through the thick door, muffled and panicked. "Don't do this!" It's definitely coming from inside this room.

I check the number once again—room 813.

*This is it.*

"Let me go!" she cries louder. Her voice is feral. Terrified. She's being hurt.

A lump forms in my throat, my heart pounding so hard I can't think straight. It's as if I've been doused with cold water.

"*Hey!*" I pound on the door.

Without a second thought, I press my key card against the card reader. When the light blinks green, I push the door open and dart inside.

*I should've called the police.* I realize it as soon as I'm in the room, but there's no time.

The woman on the bed looks up at me as if I'm her last hope. She's in her sixties, if I had to guess, and my guesses have become very accurate over the years. She appears younger than Constance, though not by much. Her white gown is torn open up to her waist, her legs spread, body draped across the bed. It's a small mercy the man on top of her hasn't gotten started with what he clearly came here to do.

He turns around at the commotion, and I take in the sight of his dark clothing and black ski mask. Only the bit of skin surrounding his blue eyes peeks out, hardly distinguishable.

The corners of his eyes wrinkle with confusion as he climbs off the bed. "Get out of here!" he bellows, waving a frantic arm at me as if I might've just stumbled into the wrong room and will be on my way now.

Perhaps that's what I should do.

Maybe a smarter man would.

Turning back to the woman, the man reaches for the gun lying on the comforter. I didn't see it at first, but it's all I can see now.

It happens in a flash. I charge at him, not thinking about myself or Willa, not thinking about anything but making him stop.

Making this end.

The woman scoots back on the bed, gathering her dress to cover herself. She's nearing hysterics as the man turns to face me.

"Stop him, please!" she shouts.

"Call 9-1-1!" I yell at her.

The man lowers the gun slightly just before I launch into him, knocking him off his feet and to the ground. The thud is muffled by the carpet covering the concrete floor.

He tries to sit up, but I slam him back down. His head rolls back, eyes blinking and unfocused. I've hit him too hard, I realize.

I grab the gun, hold it over him, and toss her my phone. "Call 9-1-1!" I shout again, realizing she still hasn't.

She's completely frozen with wide-eyed fear. A deer in the headlights. Her panic is contagious as I realize that if she calls the police, I could go to jail. I will have to explain why I'm here, why I have a room key, and I have no explanation to offer.

"Are you okay?" I ask, my heart pounding so fast in my chest it feels like it's trying to escape. I can't focus on my own worries right now. I have to protect her.

The man struggles underneath me, and I jab the gun into his throat. I have no idea what I'm doing. I've never shot a gun before and don't know if the safety is on or even how to tell.

I hope and pray he won't call my bluff.

*Click.*

I almost miss the sound in the commotion, but it's there. A familiar click I've heard so many times before. I glance over my shoulder, dread swelling in my gut, and find the woman pointing a phone in my direction. She no longer appears scared but rather happy, in fact.

No, *happy* isn't the right word either. On someone like her, happiness appears almost cruel.

I stand up off the man, keeping the gun trained on him. "Don't move," I warn him, studying her as she lowers the phone. "What are you doing? Did you just take a photo?"

Pictures are strictly off-limits for any appointment. Maddie will have made her aware of this. Clients request it all the time, but the answer is always no.

Soon enough, I want to be out of this, and photographic proof that I was ever in it will only further complicate things.

She drops the phone on the bed, trying and failing to appear innocent.

"No, of course not."

I don't know why I do it. Everything in me screams I'm in danger; everything tells me something is wrong with this situation. I lift the gun and point it at the woman.

"What's going on? Tell me."

*Click.*

I know what's happened before I can look down. But eventually, I do, and I find the man on the floor has taken another phone out and snapped a picture of me too.

"Send it," the woman says softly.

"Done."

"*What the hell is going on?*" I demand, not sure which of them to look at, which of them to point the gun at. What have I just done?

In my job, it helps to be able to read people. I've become quite good at it over the years. Expressions are often more honest than words. Even on the most dishonest people, sometimes our faces tell the truth.

By the looks on *their* faces, it seems I've played right into their hands.

The man scrambles to his feet, tucks his phone into his pocket, makes eye contact with me just once, and then turns to walk from the room without a word. From where I stand, I spy the dark blood trickling down the small piece of his neck that's exposed under the black ski mask.

"You're hurt," I call after him, though the small part of me that's worried about his well-being is quickly being overshadowed by my need to understand what's happening.

When I turn back to the woman, she's eased herself to the edge of the bed, one leg thrown over the other, her hands folded and resting on her knees. She's elegant and regal, with the kind of confidence that can only come from wealth. True wealth. Not simple richness.

Some people think there's no difference, but it couldn't be further from the truth. New money is loud, obnoxious. They never really feel like they have the money, so they make sure everyone knows they do. Underneath it all, rich people are insecure and uneasy, so they do the only thing they know to do, which is often making a scene.

Wealth is subtler. Quieter. Wealthy people have no need to prove themselves to anyone in any room. They belong simply because they always have.

Most of my clients are rich. This one, there's no doubt in my mind, is wealthy.

She studies me, smiling from behind smooth, frozen skin that could only be the result of thousands of dollars of treatments and even more in creams and skincare.

Not that I'm judging. If I could afford it, I would be a fan of the needle as much as the next person. We all just want to outrun time, don't we?

"What's going on?" I ask again, keeping my voice calm this time, despite the swelling sense of panic in my chest.

In a negotiation, the person who speaks first gives up their power. I've just given up mine, but then again, there was never any question of who holds the power in this room. Whether or not things went as planned, it was always going to be her.

She chuckles from somewhere deep in her throat. "You should sit."

My blood runs cold.

"Why?"

She smiles with the confidence of someone who's never been told *no*. "Because we need to talk, and I prefer to talk to people who are seated."

"You hired me."

She nods. "Then you should do as I tell you and *sit*."

Her command is that of which you'd give to a dog. She's looking at me as if that's all I am. Her eyes flick to the chair near the window.

Still carrying the gun, I cross the room and sink into the chair, never taking my eyes off her.

"Why did you do this?" I ask when she doesn't begin talking right away. The last ten minutes of my life feel like a blur. As if I could just wake up at any moment and find myself still in my own bed. In my own house. With my own wife. "Who are you?"

I should never have taken this job.

I should've known better.

I have a rule for a reason.

From the bed, my phone chimes.

I move to stand, but the woman is faster. She studies the screen, then drops it back down.

"Your payment is in."

I swallow. My payment. If I call the police now, I will go to jail. There's no question. I will lose the career I've sacrificed everything for.

I have no reasonable explanation for why I'm here, and Maddie has made it clear we're on our own if we're ever caught.

"I've purchased two hours of your time, Mr. Ashley. Two hours of your life. I think we can both agree I paid much more than you're worth for that."

Bitterness takes over my body, and I find myself gripping the gun tighter. Why is this happening? Why is she doing this? I was trying to help her.

"It's not loaded," she says, eyeing my hand. "Just so

you know. It was never loaded." She pauses. "Go on. Test it if you'd like."

I eye the gun. Of course it's not loaded. Of course. This has all been a setup, but why? Is it some sort of—

I freeze. All thoughts come to a complete halt.

*No.*

"Wait. What did you just call me?"

"Mr. Ashley. You *are* Hudson Ashley, are you not? Or would you prefer for me to call you Dr. Ashley?"

No one knows my name. Or what I do for work. Not Maddie. Not any of my clients. So how does this woman know who I am?

When I don't answer straight away, she goes on.

"Oh, that's right. I forgot you like to be called *Henry* while you're on the job, right? That's what Constance called you."

"How do you know who I am? What do you want?"

It's always been a fear of mine that a client will come to me as a patient. It's why I moved us out of the city and joined a practice and bought a house two hours from where I see my clients. It's also why I convinced Jake we should insist on seeing patient photos uploaded into the portal along with their medical history before we schedule their appointments.

I sold it as a safety precaution for everyone, though it's always been an unnecessary practice.

Until now.

Until someone discovered who I am.

"Relax, Mr. Ashley. I have no intentions of harming you or your perfect little wife. I just want to talk."

"Talk about what?" I point the unloaded gun in the direction of the door. "Who was that man?"

I do have clients who want to talk, strangely enough. At the end of the day, I think that's what most of them want. My clientele is primarily women in their fifties and sixties who find themselves feeling unneeded and unappreciated by their husbands and families. One told me once she went an entire week without speaking a word to her husband, and she was certain he hadn't noticed. Most of them just want someone to make them feel wanted. Loved.

It's why I make such an effort to be sure Willa always knows how much she means to me. How amazing I think she is. As much as I help my clients, they help me, too. I like to think of it as a sort of reverse therapy, though I'm sure a therapist would have a thing or two to say about that. Still, they teach me ways to be a good husband by telling me all the wrong things their husbands do. Or *don't* do, most often.

"He was one of you," she says finally. "Not quite your... What's the word? *Caliber*. Much more affordable. Then again, I wasn't sure he'd survive the night if your attack got much more violent, so I could hardly waste much money on him, could I?"

I huff out a breath, recalling the way I'd pounded the man's head on the concrete floor. With or without the carpet, it was enough to do damage. "He was a sex worker?"

"Is that what they call you?" She purses her dark-maroon-stained lips. "In my day, we just called you *whores*."

She says the word like it might sting, but it doesn't. Whatever label she wants to put on what I do, I've heard it before. There is no stigma for me. It's part of my identity, and it's given me a beautiful life that was going rather well until I walked into this hotel room.

"You hired him like you hired me. Why?"

"Yes, well, I told him we were going to have a little fun with role-play." Her lips curve into a devilish smile.

"Maddie never mentioned role-play."

She always tells me if clients have special requests, so I can be prepared or even turn things down on rare occasions.

"Well, you still played your role smashingly."

"What are you talking about?"

She picks up her phone and turns it around, scrolling through the set of photos. One, with me on top of the man on the floor, gun in my hand, shoved into his neck. The other, obviously taken by the man, with me facing the bed, glaring at the woman. The gun in my hand is pointed directly at her, my anger on full display.

Even from here, I know how bad this looks.

She feigns innocence. "I'd hate for anyone to find out you tried to attack me."

"*Attack you?* I didn't. I would never do that! I was trying to *save* you, and we both know it. I thought you were in danger." I should've just called the police and walked away, but it's too late now.

She clicks her tongue. "From the looks of these

pictures, the only danger to me...is *you*. I'm sure my little friend would agree if the police need to get involved." She points toward the door. "I can always call him back."

The police? She hasn't called them yet, but she could. Who will they believe if it's my word against hers?

On the one hand, she was yelling. Though I couldn't hear it until I reached the door, someone on the other side of the wall might have. But how would I prove it wasn't me causing her to yell?

They'd have the information from the time I used my key card, wouldn't they? But minutes are easily blurred in a tense moment. Am I willing to bet everything on that alone?

Willa would corroborate my story, but what wife wouldn't?

There won't be any of my DNA on her, but my fingerprints are all over this gun. Who knows what else this gun has been used for? And the photos are damning. She's right. If it's her word against mine and I have to tell the police I was here as an escort, there's no doubt in my mind they'll believe her, not me.

And I'll lose everything.

I lock my jaw as my face burns with rage. "Does Constance know you're doing this?"

"Constance." She laughs as if I've just told a great joke. As if this is a fucking comedy show at Zanies. "I very sincerely doubt Constance knows much about anything, to be honest."

*"What do you want?"* I repeat through gritted teeth.

"Well, it's simple really." She places the phone down,

smoothing a hand over the comforter. "I want something only you can help me with."

"Yeah? And what's that?"

She locks eyes with me, puffing out a breath. "I want a baby."

# CHAPTER TEN

## WILLA

When the front door opens and, seconds later, Hudson appears in the living room, I instantly know something is wrong. It's nothing about the way he looks. By all accounts, he looks the same as when he left. His hair is neat, his clothing isn't wrinkled or torn, and there are no marks, bruises, or blood to be seen. Still, something is off in his expression.

Sometimes, when he gets home from one of his jobs, he needs a few hours to decompress, and I'm always willing to give him that. After what he's doing for me, for us, it's the least I can do.

You probably hate me, I realize. Probably think I'm stupid or naive or psychotic for letting my husband do this.

Maybe you're right.

All I know is that I love my husband very much. Maybe more than I ever thought possible. My parents' marriage ended over financial stress. There was never enough money to make ends meet and fingers were always getting pointed, blame being placed on each other.

Keep in mind, too, that Hudson was doing this long before I came along. Long before I loved him and certainly long before I married him.

So, if this is what it takes—a few more years of this to ensure our marriage stays strong—then that's a sacrifice I'm willing to make.

Judge me all you want. You certainly wouldn't be the first to do so.

I'm just doing what I have to, same as the rest of us.

"Hi." I'm cautious with him, trying to get a read on his mood.

He looks up as if he just realized I'm here, and when he does, something sinks in my chest.

"What's wrong? Are you okay?"

He shakes his head, running a hand over his mouth mindlessly. Normally, I wait until he's showered to approach him in an attempt to prevent myself from smelling another woman's perfume, but he needs me, so I don't hesitate.

I step forward, arms outstretched, and pull him into my chest. His head rests there, the weight of the world ever present.

"What happened?"

"We need to talk."

The four most devastating words in the human language, as far as I'm concerned. I suck in a breath, trying to stay calm as he pulls back from me and sinks down on the ottoman in front of the couch. I sit across from him, clasping his hands in mine.

"What is it?"

"It was a setup."

His words hit me, and my mind goes to my worst fear. His client was an undercover cop. He's going to be arrested. But then, why hasn't he already been arrested? What's happening? Why did we ever decide this was a risk worth taking?

"She... The woman... She didn't want to hire me. She wanted to frame me."

A mixture of rage and fear fight for attention inside me. "Frame you? Frame you for what?"

When he looks up, his eyes are red-rimmed, hopeless. Whatever has happened, I want nothing more than to take the stress away from him.

To do what I can to help.

"She wants a baby."

The words suck the air from my lungs. "A what?"

"A baby."

My vision blurs as the room shifts around me. I may pass out. I kind of wish I would. "She wants you to get her pregnant?" I'm going to be sick.

His brows draw together for half a second. "What? No. No. Not from me. From... From *us*."

My hand touches my stomach without volition. I feel as if I've stepped into an alternate universe. How is this happening right now?

He takes my hand back, shaking his head. "Not *us, us*. She wants us to help her adopt a baby."

Relief overwhelms me, my cheeks heating. "Well, why didn't you just say that? You can put her in touch with the agency and—"

"I'm afraid it's not going to be that simple."

Now he looks as if he's the one trying to protect me.

"She's been trying to adopt since her husband died three years ago, but there are no agencies willing to work with her. She's in her sixties with no support system."

"What exactly does she think we're going to be able to do, then?"

He sighs with his lips pressed together. "She said she doesn't care how we do it, but she wants a baby. She's given us one week to make it happen."

"*One week?* Is she insane? The agency has had clients who've been on the waiting list for over a year! How on earth are we supposed to...to *produce* a baby for her in a week? Out of thin air? And why would we? I'm sorry, but agencies have guidelines for a reason. We allow a forty-year age gap, nothing more. It's for the good of the baby." My heart aches, both at the thought of this woman who desperately wants something she may be unable to have and for a baby who, if we make it happen, would likely lose their mother before graduating college or maybe even high school. "I'm sorry. Maybe it's not fair, but I can't change the rules. What about fostering? Would she consider that?"

"You don't get it." His tone is firm, as if he's annoyed with me. What am I missing here? "We have to get her a baby. Or..."

"Or what?"

He groans, then looks away. "Or she's going to ruin everything."

"I don't understand what you mean."

"She took a photo of me."

"A photo?" This is bad. Hudson never allows photos to be taken of him. It's a rule.

"With a gun. Standing at the end of her bed. Another with me holding a gun to a man's neck."

"I..." I'm at a loss for words. There are literally no words I could muster to force what he just said to make sense. "Is it... I mean, was it a *sex* thing?" I try not to ask many questions about what Hudson does. In the beginning, I wanted to know everything. Now, I'd just as soon rather not. As strong as I am, sometimes it's just too much for me to handle.

"No." He scowls. "It was a setup. I walked into the room, and there was another man already there. He had on a ski mask and... It looked like he was going to rape her, Willa. She was screaming. Her dress was ripped, and he was on top of her. I didn't think, I just acted."

"Wait, what do you mean? Acted how? What did you do? Did you hurt someone? How did you even get a gun?" We don't own guns, so as far as I know, he has no access to them.

"It was already there. On the bed." He puts his head in his hands. "I should've known better. I should've realized. It never crossed my mind that someone could be so evil. I just wanted to help her."

I put a hand on his arm. "What happened? Please talk to me. Explain."

He runs a hand over the leg of his pants, distracting himself. Avoiding looking me in the eye. "I knocked him to the ground. Shoved him. Then I grabbed the gun. He was trying to get up, so I held the gun to his neck and told the woman to call the police. I don't even know how it happened. It was all a rush."

The things he's describing to me feel like another reality. How is my husband capable of this? Of attacking someone? Holding a gun to another person's flesh? Even as a means of protection, I can't picture it. It just doesn't compute.

"But...I don't understand. Who was the man? What happened to him?"

"I don't know. He was another escort. I never saw his face."

"And he wasn't actually attacking her?"

"No." He puffs out a breath. "They were playing me the whole time. It was all an act."

"But how did they know you would help in the first place? Or that you wouldn't call the police?"

"I don't know." He groans. "It was all such a blur. One second, I'm walking off the elevator, thinking I know what to expect, and the next, I'm standing over the man holding a gun." He pauses, head hanging down. When he looks back up at me, I swear the sea of hopelessness reflecting back could swallow me up. "She took a picture of me, and then when I stood up to try to understand what was happening, he took another. It looks like I came in and attacked them. And it's their word against mine."

"And what? She means to blackmail you?"

His grimace is enough confirmation.

"But you could just tell the truth, then! Can't you? You could explain it—"

"Explain it to who, Willa? The police? I've already told you it would be my word against hers. Theirs, probably. And, besides that, if this story gets out, even if I don't go to prison by some miracle, I'll lose my job, my license. Everything we've worked so hard for will be gone." He snaps his fingers to demonstrate.

"Then we won't let that happen," I say quickly. "There has to be another way."

He stands, pacing the room. "No, there isn't. Or if there is, I can't, for the life of me, see it. I don't know what I'm going to do."

"We'll figure it out. Maybe if you tell Maddie, she can sort it out."

With his back to me, his head drops forward in defeat. "No. I can't. There's something else."

"What?" What can be worse than all of this?

"She knew who I was. She knew about you." My body no longer feels like mine. It's as if I've drifted up above myself, watching the scene unfold, hearing what he's saying. The words that will never make sense in a million years.

He spins back around to look at me. "I realize it sounds crazy, but I think... I think she targeted us."

"What? How? Why?"

"I don't know yet. Maybe she saw us as a means to an end. Easy targets. I can't just believe this is a coincidence.

Even if Constance referred her, no client has ever known my name before. Not even Constance."

"What does that mean, though?"

"It means we have to be careful with how we handle this." His eyes dart back and forth between mine. "It means she could be more dangerous than we realize."

I swallow.

How is this happening?

What have we gotten ourselves involved in?

What have we done?

# CHAPTER ELEVEN

## HUDSON

Every morning, there is a brief moment, another world between awake and asleep. When you still don't know your dreams aren't real and the stressors of the day have yet to find you.

Today, when I find myself in that place, I squeeze my eyes shut, wanting to prolong it, wanting to never wake up. Waking up means this is all actually happening and I'm going to have to deal with it. Waking up means accepting I have no idea how.

I roll over and tap my phone screen, pressing the button to end my blaring alarm. Beside me, Willa groans in protest, stretching out across the bed, one leg thrown over me casually.

It could be any other morning.

Except it's not.

It's today, and today is the day our life starts to crumble.

"Morning," she says, patting a hand on my chest, her

voice still peaceful and sleepy. She hasn't remembered yet, while I'm not sure I ever forgot.

I grasp her hand and kiss her fingers. Why did I take the job when it went against the rule that has kept us safe these past few years? *No new clients.* It was so simple, and yet, a single slip ruined everything.

I have to stop thinking this way.

If there is a way out, we'll find it.

But optimism comes after coffee, so for at least the next ten minutes, I'll allow myself to sulk.

I push the covers off me and slide from the bed, heading for the shower. I took one last night, but still, I feel dirty. It's the dirtiest I've ever felt without having sex.

The woman has the pictures. What will she do with them? Who will she show them to? Who will she send them to if we don't comply with her impossible demand?

Under the steady stream of scalding water, I picture my face plastered on the front page of the local paper. My clients would be devastated to learn the truth about who I am. They trust me to be professional, to keep them safe and healthy, to help them create families, to bring their children into the world, and now...this?

What was I thinking?

Why did I let it go this far?

I jolt when I spy a figure standing behind me and realize Willa has slipped into the bathroom without my notice. She strips out of her pajamas and opens the shower door. The look in her eyes is a question I don't have to answer.

She steps inside and under the stream of water, not

even bothering to adjust the temperature this time as she wraps her arms around me. We stand like that for several minutes, just breathing and existing.

Just soaking up what could be one of the last normal mornings of our lives.

"Can I meet her?" She doesn't look up as she asks the question.

"Meet her? Who? The client?"

"Yes."

Like hell am I letting that monster anywhere near Willa. "I don't think that's such a good idea."

"What choice do we have? How am I supposed to help her if I haven't even met her? My job is to protect the kids, to place them in good homes. Even if, by some miracle, I can make this happen, I can't in good conscience give a baby to someone I've never met or even spoken to. Especially when what I do know about her is so terrible."

I pull away, holding her at arm's length. "You mean you actually think you can make this work? Really?"

"No." She sighs. "Not really. If I'm being honest, I'm hoping I'll be able to make her understand why this *can't* work. But I'd like to make it seem like we're at least putting in our best effort."

My brilliant wife. Always trying to prove she can do the impossible. I can't help being in awe of her resilience, even as the world falls apart around us. "It's a nice thought, but I'm not sure she'll meet with me. And besides, even if I wanted to, I don't have a way to contact her."

Swiping water from her eyes, she pins me with a pointed stare. "How on earth are you supposed to let her know when we've found a baby, then?"

"She said she would contact me in a week."

"Well, there has to be something. Could Maddie give you her phone number? An email address? Something?"

"Yes," I say, but quickly add, "but she won't. It's a breach of trust for the clients. And for us. They aren't supposed to know who we are, remember?" I know she's frustrated with me. Hell, *I'm* frustrated with myself, but try as I might, I can't manage to come up with a solution that doesn't end with me in jail.

"Well, she already *does* know who you are, so that doesn't matter. Did she give you her name? Maybe we could try to look her up."

"She said her name was June, but she was probably lying."

"Just June? No last name?" She's disappointed. I hate disappointing her.

"Well, she wasn't exactly forthcoming with information in the first place. It was all I could get out of her. Trust me, I tried."

"And yet she wants us to help her?"

I rest a hand on the shower wall, leaning into it. "Willa, the woman is blackmailing us to get her a baby in a matter of days. I don't exactly think she's aiming to be voted Most Logical."

She stares into space, not looking at me or anything else for that matter. She's thinking. Deep within herself. Searching for an answer I'm not sure exists. "But why us?

Why would she think we'd be able to help her? Why would she target us? That's what I don't understand."

"I don't know. I wish I did. I guess because of our jobs."

She hugs me again. "It's all going to be okay."

"Yeah." I kiss her head. Somehow, someway, I'm going to make sure she's okay.

---

On my way to work, I dial Maddie's phone number from my call log. She answers almost instantly, in the same raspy voice as if I've woken her from sleep.

"Henry?"

"I need a way to get in contact with the client from last night."

"You know that's not allowed."

"I do," I say, trying to decide exactly how to explain the situation I've gotten myself in. "But I need there to be an exception made."

"Why? Did something happen?"

"You could say that."

"Henry, it's early. What do you want from me?"

"The client is attempting to blackmail me."

She's quiet for a moment. "What does she want?"

"Something I'm not willing to give her."

"What does she have on you?"

"She took pictures without permission." I decide to leave it at that. The less Maddie knows, the better for me. There's no doubt in my mind she's only asking these things to protect herself. She would turn on me in a second if it meant saving herself. I can't fault her for it. I'd likely do the same.

"Why didn't you ask for her phone to be put away?" She asks this as if I'm a child who's broken a rule.

"It was complicated. I didn't realize it was happening until it was too late."

I hear her moving around on the other end of the line, typing something on a keyboard, it sounds like. "And what are you planning to do about it?"

"I need to talk to her. See if she's willing to compromise. Come on, Maddie. Give me something."

"I'm sorry. You know the rules and how to keep yourself safe. I wish I could help, but I can't."

She doesn't, though she could, but I don't argue.

"So, what am I supposed to do?"

"Is she wanting you to hurt someone or something?"

"Not exactly," I say, coming to a stop at a red light. The asshole behind me is blaring his music so loud it's hard to hear her next sentence.

"Give her what she wants, then. It's what you're good at."

I don't take offense to what she's saying, but I'm not sure I should be flattered either. At the end of the day, I'm not sure what I expected from Maddie. She's protecting me as much as a grocery store manager would protect a cashier from being berated by an irate customer. Meaning she's not protecting me at all. It's par for the course. A hazard of the job. Any safety here is an illusion, and I always knew that. But surely something like this has happened before. I can't be the first.

"Can you at least give me Constance's phone number? They're friends, right?"

"Constance made the referral, yes, but I won't be able to give you any phone numbers, Henry. It's for everyone's safety."

"So there's nothing you can do to help?" I grip the steering wheel with my free hand, slamming on the gas as the light changes to green.

"'Fraid not, no. But I will block her from our list so she can't book with anyone else."

The measly act does nothing to help me feel better. Something tells me June won't be booking with anyone else anyway, so it's pointless.

It was me she wanted, and I played right into her hand.

Now, I just have to find out who she really is.

# CHAPTER TWELVE

## WILLA

When I arrive at work, I place a delivery order from Murphy's favorite doughnut shop and send her a text to let her know they're on the way.

> Thinking of you this morning. Breakfast is on me. How are you feeling?

It's another hour before she replies with a photo of the doughnut box, a short message, and a drooling emoji.

> Better now. Have I mentioned I love you?

I make it three hours into my workday before the idea hits me. If June wants to adopt so badly, surely she's already explored her options—the legal ones, I mean—before resorting to blackmailing my husband into commandeering a child for her.

With very little to go on, I open our database and type in her first name.

## June

It's all I have to go on. I hold my breath and press the button to begin the search.

There are thirty-six results for the name June, but I'm able to narrow it down based on families who have already been matched, which is most of them; families who are actively being shown to birth mothers, two of them; and families who weren't approved, just one.

*June Cromwell.*

At the time of her application, which was two years ago, she was sixty-three and recently widowed. The owner of a real estate company whose name I recognize and cofounder of a medical spa in the wealthiest part of town.

The photos she submitted make her seem normal. Sane. She's beautiful, actually. The kind of woman who brings with her a sense of peace. She seems so put together it practically takes my breath away.

This can't be her, and yet, it's too perfect a match to be anyone else.

I glance at the name on her file as I print it out: **Starla March**. My manager.

Starla has been with the company since before I graduated and has the biggest heart for this work I've ever seen. She's tough but fair, and I've seen her do the impossible for our families. If she didn't approve June's application, it wasn't without cause, and I doubt very much I'll be able to change her mind.

I wonder if she even remembers June.

If so, maybe I can get some answers.

Deciding it's worth a shot, I exit my office and head down the hall. As the manager of our small team, Starla has one of the biggest offices here, and when I stop in front of it, I'm not surprised to find the door open.

She looks up with a worried expression, probably at the sound of my footsteps, which seem to echo on the linoleum. When she sees me, the lines on her face smooth out and she pops a piece of croissant in her mouth.

"Hey, dollface. What's up?"

"I was wondering if I could ask you about an old application."

"Why sure," she drawls, dusting the crumbs from her hands and wiping the corners of her mouth before she takes the stack of papers from me. "Hmm... June Cromwell." She clicks her tongue as she reads it over. I know the instant the recollection hits her as her eyes light up. "Oh yes. I remember Ms. June. *Cromwell*, like on *Halloweentown*. My granddaughters used to love that movie." She chuckles, then looks back up at me with an incredulous expression. "Well, I'll tell you what I can. What do you want to know?"

"Um, do you remember why her application was denied?"

"Oh, sure. She was a real sweetheart, you know, but I mean, she would've been *sixty-three* years older than any infant I could've placed with her. Even if we'd accepted her and placed her with our waiting families, we both know she wouldn't have been chosen. I tried to explain it to her as gently as possible. Even offered to help her look into adopting an older child, but she wouldn't hear it. I got the feeling she isn't used to hearing the word *no*, you know what I mean?"

Not exactly what I was hoping to hear, but of course Starla already covered everything I was planning to try. She'd be a less-than-ideal candidate even for older-child adoption, but it would be possible, at least.

"Mm-hmm, I know exactly what you mean, unfortunately. So, what happened? She just left? You never heard from her again?"

"*Well*"—she draws the word out hesitantly—"there was no *just* to it. She left when we couldn't approve her application, promising to be back to sue the pants off the agency. We heard from her a few more times, mostly phone calls asking if we'd change our minds and promising we'd hear from her lawyer, but nothing ever came from it."

"You think she didn't have a case?"

"I think it just wasn't worth her time. I have no doubts she could've sued us and most likely won, but it wasn't money she was after. She wanted a baby. A lawsuit would've been a distraction. She probably went on to other agencies, probably found more than one that agreed to list her, knowing full well they were taking her money and making promises they couldn't keep. I could've done the same thing." She sighs and doesn't need to say the rest of it out loud. She could've done the same thing, but she wouldn't. Above all else, Starla truly cares about our clients. It's never been about the money for her. She wants to create families. My eyes fall on the family portrait on her desk: four happy kids, two loving parents. Next to it, a picture of her sixteen grandchildren last Christmas. She wants everyone to have what she has.

"Is there a reason you're asking about her? Has she stopped by again? Put in another application?"

I think quickly. "Yeah, she called and wanted to see about coming in to fill out an application. I told her she could do it online, but she said it was giving her an error message. When I tried to check it out, I realized it was because she was already in the system."

"Don't waste your time, girlie. She already knows the answer and it won't change. Do you need me to call and speak to her?"

"No, it's okay. I'll handle it."

"Thanks. Let me know if you need backup. June Cromwell is one of the reasons this place finally got caller ID." She releases a drawn-out sigh, then lights up again. "Oh. Speaking of applications, how did the meeting with the Hernandezes go?"

"Excellent. They're going to be a great fit for Sarah."

"I thought so too. Sweet family." Her smile is whimsical, already moving on from the conversation about June.

I take a step back, picking up June Cromwell's file on my way. "Well, I should get back to my office. I just wanted to check in with you about her."

"Sure thing." She tears off a piece of the croissant again. "Pastries in the break room, by the way."

Back in my office, I skim through the files again,

learning all I can about the woman who seems hell-bent on ruining my life. Is that why she's doing this? Because our agency turned her down? If so, why not target Starla, rather than me?

Then again, Hudson's side job makes us vulnerable in a way Starla's accountant husband could never be.

With nothing left to lose, I make the decision that may very well haunt me forever. I pick up my phone and dial her number.

"June Cromwell."

She's the type of woman who answers the phone with simply her name. No greeting. No sense of warmth.

"Hello, June. This is Willa Ashley calling from—"

"Yes, I know who you are, Mrs. Ashley." She rolls the words slowly over her tongue, as if tasting each syllable. "It's very ballsy of you to call me yourself, I have to say. I wondered who would reach out first."

I swallow. "You were expecting my call?" I'm not sure if she thinks I'm calling for the agency or for my husband.

"Yes, well, I assume you want to discuss the little deal I made with your husband last night."

Found my answer. "I—"

"Tell you what, let's all meet at Etch at noon, shall we?"

"What? You mean today?"

She chuckles under her breath, a sound that feels like nails on a chalkboard to my brain. "Unless you have something more important to do?"

"No. Fine. Noon. Gr—"

She ends the call before I can finish my sentence. "Great. Nice talking with you too," I say to myself, placing the phone down with extra oomph.

Just like that, I'm all set to meet the woman who dropped the match and set my world on fire.

# CHAPTER THIRTEEN

## HUDSON

"This is a bad idea."

Willa has barely rounded the corner to meet me in front of the restaurant before I begin chiding her. I couldn't say much on the phone, surrounded by my team, and I couldn't excuse myself to my office because the IT department was upgrading our software and security systems. New cameras everywhere except the exam rooms which upload footage directly to the cloud will provide top-notch security, but pretty much negate any semblance of the privacy we once had.

So, I'll say what I need to say now. "You have no idea what you're walking into. We have no plan. No time to prepare."

"I understand all of that, but we have to do something. I talked to Starla about her—"

*"You told Starla about all of this?"* I whisper-shout, tugging her off to the side of the restaurant's entrance, past an oversized potted plant.

"Of course not. Not about *this*." She waves a hand back and forth between our chests. "I told her June had called in and wanted to place an application again."

"*Again?* What do you mean? How does she know who June is?"

"She applied to adopt through us before. A few years ago. Apparently, she wasn't happy with Starla when she told her it wasn't likely to happen."

A piece of the puzzle slips into place for me, but I hold it in as a group of people dressed in suits move past us. I lower my voice. "So that's how you found out how to contact her?"

She nods, checking over her shoulder. "Her phone number was on file, yes. I found out quite a lot about her, actually."

"Like what?"

Normally, I would never ask about clients of my wife's agency, and even if I did, she would never share. Then again, this entire scenario is the epitome of *ab*normal. I need to know what we're dealing with.

"Well, I have her address, which is in Brentwood. Her husband passed away three years ago, which was around the time she started trying to adopt. And she owns several businesses around town, the most lucrative of which are a real estate company and a medical spa in Green Hills, so she's ridiculously rich. Powerful," she adds, almost as an afterthought, as if she doesn't think I'm getting what she's saying. "Based on everything I read, she's very, very powerful."

"Well, great." My words drip with sarcasm. "That all sounds promising."

"Yes, it's not good, but there has to be a reason she wants this baby, Hudson. Something deeper. Why now? And why us? Why is she willing to go through all of this?"

"She's not used to being told no."

"Yeah, that's what you said." Willa hesitates. "It's funny... Starla said the same thing."

A bitter lump forms in my throat. "Someone wealthy and powerful like that, maybe her husband never wanted kids. Now that he's out of the picture and she finally has her chance, everyone's telling her no anyway. I'd imagine she doesn't like that very much." I can see it so clearly now, her willingness to do anything required to get what she wants. Lie, blackmail, kill.

Over her shoulder, something catches my eye. When I glance up, I spy June stepping out of a town car. She waves at the driver, rushing him away, before setting her sights on us.

At noon, the woman looks ready for an extravagant night out, dressed in a black sequin blazer, slacks, and red heels. There's something off about her smile, something about the warmth that doesn't reach her eyes.

She stops in front of us. "Hello again, Mr. Ashley."

At this point, I have to wonder if she's deliberately not calling me *Dr.* Ashley just to make a point.

"This is my wife"—I gesture toward her—"Willa."

"I would say it's nice to meet you, but I think we both know it'd be a lie." June looks toward the door as Willa tucks a strand of blonde hair behind her ear, tugging at it a bit more than necessary to hide her frustration.

"Agreed," Willa says.

"Shall we go in? I made a reservation, and I'd hate to be late."

Without waiting for an answer, she heads for the door and stops short in front of it. I'm not sure what she's waiting for, but finally, Willa reaches for the handle. Realizing what's happening, I pull it from her grasp, holding the heavy wood-and-glass door open for the both of them.

"Thank you." Willa meets my eyes for half a second as she passes through the doorway and follows June into the restaurant.

Minutes later, we're sitting at what could arguably be called the best table in the house. I wonder what strings June had to pull to get us in here on such short notice.

"Well, I guess we should just get right to it, shouldn't we?" She folds her hands together, resting them on the table after the waiter disappears to get our drinks.

The tables here are close together—close enough I know the two women sitting next to us are coworkers who seem not to like each other all that much.

"Yes." Willa keeps her voice low. "Thank you for agreeing to meet with us on such short notice. I—"

"Well, of course. Anything for my two miracle workers." Again with the cool smile. "Frankly, I'm shocked it took you this long to call."

"It's been twelve hours," I point out.

She wiggles her shoulders. "Time is ticking."

"Exactly, which is why I thought we could talk about what it is you're asking," Willa says.

"Mr. Ashley didn't tell you?" She feigns shock.

"He did," she assures her. "But I wanted to talk it over in person. I spoke to my supervisor, who told me she's already spoken with you quite extensively about our process and why it may be difficult to place a newborn in your care."

"Yes." The word is as sharp as a knife. "Which is why I never mentioned your agency."

"Right, but I'm afraid that answer hasn't changed. I don't want you to be discouraged, though. My job is to help people achieve their dreams of building a family, and I take great pride in that. While I know you would prefer to adopt an infant, I really think we should discuss older-child adoption. There are plenty of children in foster care who need loving homes—"

"Yes, yes, and I'm sure you'll make sure they get them—"

"I actually don't work with—"

"Just not with me."

We pause as the waiter returns with our drinks and asks if we're ready to order. It's only now I realize we haven't even looked at our menus.

Quickly, we each place our orders. I choose the first thing I see, as I don't have much of an appetite anyway, and he disappears again.

"June, I really think—"

"No, no, no, no, no." She wags a finger. "I'm not

asking you to *think*. I'm asking you to *do*. *Do* get me a child. *Do* make this work for all of us."

"All due respect..." Willa is barely holding it together right now, and though I know I need to jump in, I have no idea what to say.

*This was a bad idea.* The realization keeps floating through my head.

In tense situations, people tend to fight, run, or freeze. It's the old fight-or-flight theory. My wife is choosing to fight, while I, despite my best efforts, despite my very nature, can't seem to get myself unfrozen.

"I can't just"—Willa checks over her shoulder and lowers her voice further—"*produce* a baby out of thin air. If you want a child, we have options, but you have to work with me."

"I don't think I do," June says. "In fact, I know I don't. Unless you're prepared to have me go to the police."

She's too loud. The couple at the table behind her glance our way.

"No, of course not," I say, gripping Willa's hand on the tabletop. "But what's to stop you from doing that in the future anyway? How do we know you won't still try to hurt us once we've given you what you want?"

She thinks for a moment. "You don't, I guess. You have nothing but my word, which likely doesn't mean much to you. But what I can tell you, what I can assure you, is that I am nothing if not a woman of my word. Once I have the baby, I will be on my way and you will never hear from me again."

I twirl my drink on the table, trying and failing to ease my growing frustration. "We just want to understand what exactly you'd like us to do. How we're supposed to pull this off. We aren't miracle workers, June." I recall her words. "We're just people. What are we supposed to do?"

"Do whatever you have to do." She waves a hand in the air casually, like it's the least of her concerns. "Whatever it takes. If anyone can help me, I have full faith it will be you. You work with pregnant women every day, don't you, Mr., oh, excuse me, *Dr.* Ashley? As do you, Willa. Who is better equipped to find a child who needs a better home than you two? I couldn't have chosen better jobs for you myself. What's the problem?"

"The problem is it's not that simple," I tell her.

"Oh." She purses her lips, laughing away our concerns. "Nonsense."

"June, have you thought about hiring a surrogate instead of pursuing adoption?" Willa asks.

"Briefly, yes. I spoke to a few of those agencies when the adoption agencies turned me down. I was told it wasn't an option."

"Yes, but there's always private surrogacy." Willa lowers her voice. "I could help you find someone who would be willing to accept payment under the table, perhaps."

"No. I don't want to go through that. I won't."

"Surely you have the money to hire, like, fifty surrogates. Why won't you at least try?"

June stiffens in her seat. "As I have said, I have tried. I'm done trying. Surrogacy is not an option, and I'm sure anyone willing to accept payment under the table will no doubt be less than quality. No, I want you to find me the best of the best. Someone who has approached your agency to do the right thing. Someone who will give me a perfect child."

"They would have to meet you. They would have to agree that you're the right fit for their child."

Willa doesn't have to say the rest out loud: the likelihood of that happening is as close to zero as it gets.

"There are ways around that, aren't there? Surely you can find someone uninterested in meeting the adoptive parent? Or find a mother who you think is unfit? Convince her to give the child up?"

"How would that be different than surrogacy?"

June purses her lips. "I've told you I'm not interested in surrogacy. I considered it in the past, but had no luck. It's too late now. Finding someone worthy, waiting to see if the pregnancy will actually take, then waiting another nine months? No, thank you. In case you hadn't realized, I'm not getting any younger. I want a baby soon."

Sighing, Willa goes on, "Any birth mother, regardless of whether she wants an open or closed adoption, would likely still want to see pictures of you, June. To know who you are. It isn't as simple as what you're suggesting."

"So, tell them I'm someone else," she says. "How would they know?"

"What you're suggesting is essentially"—Willa mouths the next word—"*kidnapping*. We can't just decide which children need new homes. We can't override birth families' decisions. Any baby I have access to has to be placed into an adoptive family by choice of the birth mother or birth family."

"Well, as I said, I'm not married to any certain way of doing things. I don't need to know the details." June swirls the black straw around in her drink, looking out the window as if it's a regular day. As if this is just another Tuesday for her. "I have full faith you'll get it done. After all"—she leans down, lifting the straw toward her lips— "it's not as if you have a choice, do you?"

Willa grips my hand tighter, the conversation over.

Without another word, I pull her to her feet, toss enough cash to cover our bill onto the table, and we leave the restaurant.

"There's always a choice," I whisper, lying through my teeth when we're far enough away I can breathe again. "We just have to find ours."

# CHAPTER FOURTEEN

## WILLA

When the door opens that afternoon, I expect to see Hudson coming in from work, but instead, it's Murphy standing there. I take in the sight of her bloodshot, tired eyes. She's obviously been crying.

"What is it? What's wrong?" I glance at her stomach, hidden beneath her favorite Schrute Farms hoodie, for some indication, though it's silly, I realize in afterthought.

"Nothing," she insists. "Sorry. I just... I needed to *not* be at home right now."

She doesn't need to say what she really means for me to understand it. *Needed to not be alone.*

"Sure. No problem. I was just waiting on Hudson to get home so we could figure out dinner. Do you want to stay and eat? We could order in."

"Do you mind?" She's already sitting down on the couch when she asks. It's more of a nicety, after all. Murphy always has and always will be welcome here.

She's the sister I never had, and for as long as I can remember, we've been a package deal.

"Of course not. I'd offer you some wine, but I guess we can't do that anymore, hmm? I keep forgetting. What about tea? I just got a new peppermint."

"Tea me, babe," she says casually, grabbing the remote from where it rests on the end table closest to her and scrolling through our various streaming subscriptions.

When I return several minutes later with mugs in hand, she's crying again—trying and failing to hide it. She runs her hand through her shoulder-length hair—the strawberry-blonde waves I've always been envious of.

I sit down next to her after placing our teas on the end tables. "Okay. What's going on? Talk to me. Is everything okay with the baby?"

She uses both hands to dry under her eyes. "Yes, ugh. Why can't I stop crying lately? I hate this."

"Because you're growing another little human in there." I poke her belly playfully. "It's normal to cry."

"Nothing about any of this is normal." She lifts her legs before dropping them on the ottoman. "I'm falling apart, Wills. I'm falling apart and throwing up twenty-seven thousand times a day while simultaneously starving. Meanwhile, this thing is only the size of a peach and it's already pressing on my bladder enough that I wake up in pain from holding my pee in so much. And when I asked my doctor about it, he just said not to hold it for so long, but like, what am I supposed to do, set a pee alarm? I can't help it if I don't wake up because I'm exhausted!"

She's crying again. "And when I do wake up, I just throw up, so then I'm throwing up and peeing and also craving cheesecake. How is any of this normal? Why doesn't anyone warn us about this? Why aren't there women in the streets screaming about how awful pregnancy is?"

I cover my laugh with a cough, though I suspect I've done a bad job. "Because"—I pull her into a one-armed hug, settling into the couch—"the second you hold that baby in your arms, you forget all about how bad it is."

"Is that true?" She eyes me, and I dry her cheeks with the back of my hand.

"That's what they say in the brochures."

She laughs through her tears, shaking her head. "Well, those brochures were clearly written by men."

"Maybe so." I squeeze her tighter, then meet her eyes. "You know you don't have to do this, right?"

"I know."

I pull back. "No, I'm serious. I know you've said you don't want to talk about it, but we have to talk about it. It's not going away, Murph. This is real. It's getting more real by the day."

"I know that."

My eyes bounce back and forth between hers. Why won't she open up to me? I won't pretend to understand how she feels, but this is what I do. I can help her if she'll just let me. "If you don't want to go through with this pregnancy, say the word. You're how far along again?"

"Fourteen weeks," she reminds me.

I do the mental math. "So we'd have to go out of state

to have the procedure, but I will drive you myself. We can get a hotel room, and I'll take care of you. You're not in this alone. Never have been, never will be."

She's still for a moment as if she's been waiting to hear these exact words. Waiting for permission to feel what she's feeling.

"I know."

"I mean it. I'm here for whatever you decide."

"I know, Wills. I promise."

I give her a lopsided grin and pull her into my shoulder again. "And if you decide to have this baby, I will be here with adult diapers and puke bags, ready to be the best godmother ever."

At that, she laughs. An honest, caught-off-guard laugh that reminds me of simpler times. "Just be sure you get those cute adult diapers, the ones with the lace."

"Lacy adult diapers. Got it."

She nuzzles into my shoulder a bit more, and we've just started an episode of *Queer Eye* when she speaks again.

"What if I wanted to put the baby up for adoption?"

I pause the show, turning to face her. My lungs have steeled at the question. "Is that something you're considering?"

I know we're the same age, and I will fight anyone for even suggesting she's not a strong, capable woman, but at this moment, she looks so fragile and unsure that I would do anything to make this okay for her. "You could help me, couldn't you?"

"Of course I could, Murph. Of course. We could find this baby an amazing family if that's your choice."

She nods slowly, contemplating. "How does it work?"

All the years we've known each other, we've never really talked about my job. She knows what I do in theory, but that's about the extent of it.

"Well, for starters, we would talk it through. You and me. I could tell you what to expect and answer any of your questions. Then if you decide you want to move forward, we'd discuss what type of adoptive family you'd hope for. You can get as specific as you want. We could look through profiles of the families we already have approved and ready. They've all written letters, and most of them have photo books we keep at the office. You can narrow it down to just one or as many as you'd like. Or, if none of them jump out at you, we'll keep looking. When you find one you'd like to meet, we can set up an interview at the office, or you could go to dinner, coffee... The ball is really in your court."

"Would the baby know about me?" Her voice is so small I want to wrap her in a hug, but I refrain.

Right now, she just needs answers. Options. I've tried my hardest not to push, to just be here for her however I can, but I want to do more. To help her somehow in a way that isn't checking in and sending food. Maybe this is my chance.

"That would be up to you and the adoptive parents. But ultimately, you. If you want the baby to know about you, or if you even wanted to keep the door open for communication or visits, we'd find parents interested in an open adoption."

"Okay." She nods, turning her head back to the TV. I can't tell what she's thinking. "Okay," she repeats. Then she grabs the remote and presses play.

I hate myself for the words repeating in my head: *This could be the way.*

# CHAPTER FIFTEEN

## HUDSON

The next morning, I lean across the bed and press my lips to Willa's forehead. She stirs, rolling onto her side with her hand shielding her eyes.

"Morning, sleepyhead."

She opens one eye, grunting at me with displeasure. I smile, though her eyes are closed again, so she doesn't notice.

I worked late last night on a surprise delivery for a patient whose labor started two weeks early, so I didn't see much of her, but when I did come home, she was already in bed, watching TV, and she seemed *off*.

I'm assuming it's because of the lunch with June, and I can't blame her for that. I just hope that's all there is to it.

"I'm heading in. I have a few errands to run before work. Are you up?" I check the time. My wife, god love her, is not a morning person. She can stay awake as late as she needs, but try to wake her up an hour early and you're in for a fight.

Usually, I bring her coffee in the morning and make sure she's actually awake enough before I leave. If I don't get assurances she's awake, there's a good chance she'll fall back asleep the instant I leave the house and end up late for work.

It's happened more than a few times.

"Willa, honey. You awake?"

No answer.

I lean down, jostling her under the covers and pressing another kiss to her temple. "Wake up, beautiful. I'm leaving for work."

Both eyes open this time, and she stares at me as if she doesn't know who I am for half a second, then seems to register what's happening. She stretches, running her hands over her eyes with a loud yawn.

"You're going to work now? What time is it?"

"Early. I have a few errands to run before I head in."

She eyes me for a second. "Okay."

"Sorry I got home so late." I told her as much last night, but I need to say it again. Need her to hear it. Especially now.

"It's not your fault. How's your patient?"

"Healthy. Baby's good."

She nods but seems out of it. Lost in thought. I hate that I've done this to her. I can't help blaming myself, though I know she never would. I start to walk out of the room, but something in her eyes has me hesitating. I turn back to face her. "It's all going to be fine. It'll work out somehow. You know that, right?"

She forces a smile that anyone else might buy. "Yeah. I know."

"Is there something else wrong?"

When she meets my eyes, I know I've nailed it. Something else is happening.

"What is it?"

She opens her mouth but lets it hang open for a while like she's mentally testing what she's going to say next. "Murphy came by for dinner last night."

No.

The baby.

Has she lost it? Why didn't Willa mention anything?

"Is she okay?" I'm almost scared to ask.

"She's considering putting the baby up for adoption."

A range of emotions swims through me. Sadness, confusion, *hope*. The last one burns as if I've been stung by a swarm of bees from the inside.

"She said that? Why?"

"Because she isn't ready. She was never ready. It's not like this was planned." She looks up at me, silently begging me not to judge her for what she says next. "To be honest, I think it's the right choice."

I don't agree. Can't. It's not my place. Murphy is like Willa's sister, and if there's one thing I've learned over the years, it's that Willa can say what she wants to about her, but that privilege isn't afforded to me. "Then why the face?"

"Well." The word is a full sentence, and the pause

that awaits is a loud, ticking clock in my ears. When she finally looks up at me, it's with a steely, uneasy gaze. "We need a baby, and now, we might have one."

Everything goes fuzzy as I take in what she's implying. I hate that we've shared the same thought. "You want to give Murphy's baby to June?"

She purses her lips, annoyed. More with herself than me. I know her well enough to understand how much she hates herself for the suggestion. "I don't want to give June *anyone's* baby, least of all my best friend's. I don't want to be in this mess in the first place. But what choice do we have? You said it yourself, there's always a choice. A way out. We just have to find it."

She looks down, folding her arms over herself. "We need a baby, and I have no idea where we're going to get one. Starla will never approve her for adoption, and she's unwilling to consider an older child. She said no to surrogacy and we can't kidnap a child. If we refuse to do anything, refuse to give her what she wants, you go to jail. If we say no, we lose everything."

She's right, and I hate it. Mostly because I'm not sure she'll ever forgive me for this. I know her. I understand what's unsaid here, the silent truths staining this moment like oil. Impossible to ignore or wash out.

Even though she's suggesting it, it's not what she wants. What Murphy decides to do with the baby should be between her and the father, but bringing June into this isn't a solution I want to accept.

At least, not until we have no option left.

I sink down on my knees next to the bed and reach

for her hands, pulling them to my lips. "We are not going to lose everything. I won't let it happen."

"Then what, Hudson? Because I don't see a way out. She won't listen to reason, won't consider an older child or surrogacy, so we have no viable solutions. This is the only way. Any pregnant mother that comes in through the agency will be on record. Murphy isn't in our system yet. It would be easy enough to do."

Of course, she's speaking logistically, not emotionally.

"It's not the only way. I promise you. There's always a way. *Another* way. There has to be. Neither of us is in the business of giving up. Our clients and patients count on us to find solutions when they've run out, right?"

"Right."

I squeeze her hands gently. "I don't want you to worry about this. I'm going to handle it. I promise."

"You're not in this alone," she says softly. "I won't let you be."

"I love you." I brush her nose with mine and stand from the floor. "I have to go. Have a good day, okay?"

"You too."

She doesn't say anything else as I leave. As much as I want to stay and comfort her, to talk through this again, to promise her everything will be okay, I have to go.

I got Willa into this mess. It was my decision to enter this world when I fully understood the risks.

Before me, she went about things the right way, the safe way. I was the one who convinced her this would all be okay when we needed extra money years ago, and that's why I have to make it okay now.

I ponder our situation as I make my way out the door and into the car with a newfound determination to fix this, no matter the cost.

That's why, when I should turn right to get to my office downtown, I turn left instead.

Last night, after I arrived home, I carefully combed through the file on June that Willa had retrieved from work, trying to find anything we might be able to use against her.

While I didn't find anything particularly useful, I did find her address.

I pull up in front of the estate within twenty minutes. It's beautiful, though I'd expect nothing less, with sprawling dogwood trees across the front yard to provide what privacy the gate does not. From what I can see, it's a three-story, white colonial.

Much too big for one person.

I try to find sympathy in myself for this woman and what she's been through. I'm not heartless. I know hurt people hurt people, and I understand she's gone through a terrible loss. The idea of ever losing Willa is enough to bring me to my knees. I'd never leave the house again. Never want to eat again. Shower. Live.

I don't see how it would be possible to carry on.

But, try as I might, I have no sympathy for her. She may have lost her husband, but that is not on us. We've done nothing wrong, and yet, she's hell-bent on destroying us. We weren't hurting anyone. We didn't do anything to her. We were living our lives, and she chose us. Chose to destroy us. To ruin everything.

A rap at my window causes me to jolt, and when I look up, panic courses through me. June stands there, dressed to the nines at an hour that feels too early for anyone normal to be awake. She wiggles her fingers at me as I roll down the window.

"Can I help you?"

"Why are you doing this?" I demand, speaking before I've had time to prepare my thoughts.

She crosses her arms, tapping a finger against her bicep. "We've been over this, Mr. Ashley. You know why. I want something, and you're the only person who can help me to get it."

"I hardly think I'm the only person who can help you. There are agencies out there who do this. Who help people adopt children. I'm just one person. Willa's agency is just one agency. Find another."

She clicks her tongue. "Oh. You're a very powerful person. Don't sell yourself short."

"Yeah, so powerful I'm flat on my back every month to make ends meet."

She scoffs, rubbing her hands over her arms to ward off a shiver as the wind picks up. She brushes a piece of hair from her eyes, her long, black fingernails catching my attention. They're fitting somehow. She looks like a witch. "Now is not the time for a pity party."

"Funny, I didn't think you knew what pity was."

She glowers at me. "You and I both know you could walk away from that life if you wanted to."

"You know nothing about me." I want to lunge at her,

the urge as real as if I were a dog that smelled fresh meat. This woman makes me feral.

*I want her to die.*

The thought has bile rising in my throat. I hate myself for thinking it. I hate who she's turning me into.

"I wouldn't be so sure about that. Knowledge is power, and I am very, very powerful." She lets the words and their implications linger. "Now, I need to get back to work, and you need to stop casing my house like a common criminal."

I glance at the house next door—equally big, equally nice. "What? Don't want the neighbors to see you with an escort?"

She laughs, following my gaze. "I couldn't care less what my neighbors see. I promise I wouldn't be the first on this block to hire someone like you. But right now, you have things to do."

"How am I supposed to get you a baby?" I shout.

She's unfazed. "I guess you'll have to get creative. And your time is running out, so you'd better work fast." She steps forward, lowering her voice as if telling me a secret. "What would people say if they found out your pretty, little wife is okay with what you do? That she encourages it, even. People wouldn't like it, I'd be willing to bet. The world tends to be much less forgiving of women, you know. It won't be you they hate."

The truth in her words stings. I refuse to let Willa take the fall for this. Something clenches inside me as she starts to walk away. I can't let her go. I need to think of something. Anything.

*"What if we need months?"*

She turns back to face me, a silver eyebrow quirked. "Months?"

"We..." I hate myself for the words about to leave my mouth. "We might know how to get you a baby, but the woman's just a few months along. Fourteen weeks. The baby won't be here for a while. It would be months before we could deliver it to you."

She seems to weigh her options. "Who's the woman? A client at the agency?"

"Yes," I lie.

Her head tilts to this side, then that. Finally, she gives a firm nod. "Alright, if you could guarantee me a baby, I'd be willing to wait." She takes another step toward me. "But don't think you can do this to buy time. I'd need assurances. Updates. Ultrasounds."

"Of course."

She dips her head slightly. "If you can get me a baby, Mr. Ashley, *promise me* a baby, I will wait months."

With that, she's gone and I have no idea what I've just done.

# CHAPTER SIXTEEN

### WILLA

I text Starla and let her know I will be late for work this morning before calling June. If Hudson knew I was planning to meet with her, especially alone, I have no doubt he'd be furious. But I need to act now, before my nerves get the best of me and I decide I can't do this.

She agrees to meet me in public, and we land on the library as an ideal spot. The second floor of the parking garage to the library, more specifically.

When June arrives, she's being driven in the same black town car that brought her to lunch yesterday. Though I'd initially—*ridiculously*—assumed she'd taken an Uber, I now realize this must be her driver.

She waits for me to step out of my car before she does. When her eyes land on me, she grimaces. "You know, I'm starting to get a little bit annoyed with all the hand-holding required. Here I thought you guys were self-starters."

I shove my hand into my jacket pocket, checking for the phone that is set to record.

*Deep inhale.*

*Go.*

"I just want to know why you're blackmailing us, June."

She's quiet for a moment. Steady. Still. As if reading a menu. She opens her mouth, then closes it again.

"What on earth are you talking about?"

I squeeze my hands into fists. "Why are you doing this? Why do you want a baby so badly, anyway?"

"Well, you're in the business of creating families. Isn't that what you said to me? I thought you'd be excited to have a new client. Especially given your financial predicament. Given that your husband has to sell his body illegally for money, I'm assuming you're looking to get promoted. I was trying to help you."

The feigned ignorance on her face is repulsive. She knows what's happening. She knows what she's done. The audio in my pocket is now unusable. My heartbeat thuds in my ears, my face too hot.

Maybe I can edit the recording, though. Somehow.

I press her again.

"You're not a client. You're blackmailing us to do what you want. To deliver you a baby like we're a courier."

"Is that what you consider yourself? A courier? Honestly, Willa, have some respect for what you do. I have no idea what you're calling blackmail. I'm trying to give a child a home. If your agency won't work with me, fine. Just say that. There's no reason for this, quite frankly, aggressive dressing down in the parking lot. *You* asked *me* to meet you, not the other way around."

I groan. "We don't want to do this, June."

"And, as we discussed, if you don't, I will move forward in the only way I know how."

"By trying to destroy my family."

She's silent.

"Why?" I demand. "What have we ever done to you?"

"Are you feeling alright, Willa? You're not making any sense."

The driver's door to her car opens and the driver steps out. He's tall and beefy, with cold, lifeless eyes and thick, gray hair. He looks as if he could snap me in half without breaking a sweat.

"Why are you doing this?" I beg, focusing on June rather than my fear.

He steps toward me, one hand outstretched. "You do look unwell, Mrs. Ashley. Can I take your coat for you? Take some weight off what must be an *awfully heavy pocket*?"

I freeze, terror coursing through me.

To my relief, he steps back as June turns away.

"Come on. Let's not waste our time. We really need to be going. I have an appointment. You should get some rest, dear. Perhaps they're overworking you at that place. Maybe a nice spa day would do you some good."

With that, she slips into the back seat of her car, and he closes the door with a final, menacing look my way. I don't think I breathe until they ease out of the parking lot. The driver barely looks at me as they pass. Before, I wondered if he knew what kind of monster his boss is. Now, I have no doubt.

I suppose it should've been obvious. He'd never break ranks to help me. People like June require loyalty above all else. I'd imagine he's paid very well to overlook and even assist with her dirty deeds.

When she's gone, I pull out my phone and stare down at the dark screen, a red line running across it to let me know it's still recording the silence.

It was a long shot, to begin with, but for a second, I actually believed it might work. Now, I have no idea what we're going to do.

I only know time is running out.

# CHAPTER SEVENTEEN

## HUDSON

"Hey, honey." I find my wife in the laundry room when I get home and plant a kiss on the side of her head. "How was your day?"

"It was fine." She passes an armful of damp clothes from the washer to the dryer.

"Just fine?" I stare at her. "Didn't you have a meeting between that family you liked and the birth mother?"

She nods ever so slightly, but it's as if she's not listening to a word I'm saying.

"Willa?"

Her name seems to bring her back to reality, and she glances up at me. Her eyes are bloodshot and glassy. She's been crying.

I reach for her arms. "What's wrong? Is everything okay?"

She laughs under her breath, continuing to transfer the clothes. "It's like you keep forgetting about what's happening."

My heart sinks. *I'm* not forgetting, I just wish *she* would. I wish she'd never been burdened with this.

"Of course I'm not forgetting. I just... Some things have to stay normal between us. I need that. You need that. We're dealing with a terrible thing, a terrible person, and I know it's stressful, but we will make it through this."

She slams the door to the dryer closed and starts it up, dropping her head.

"Do you honestly believe that? Or is it just what you feel like you're supposed to say? Be real with me, Hudson. Please. I can't take any more lies."

I bat back tears of my own when she looks at me as I prepare to say the most real thing in my head. "I'm so terrified this will be the reason you leave me."

She crumples inward, her shoulders slumping as she leans forward, resting her forehead against my chest. "I'm not going to leave you," she says in a single breath. "I'm terrified you won't have a choice but to leave me."

"I went to see her today—" We both say the words at the same time.

Shock hits me square in the chest.

"You what?" I demand.

"I was trying to—"

A knock on the door interrupts us. I glance down the hall, swallowing, then back at her. "Are we expecting anyone?"

*Please say Murphy, please say Murphy, please say Murph—*

"No."

I brace myself for the worst as I head for the door. It's the police here with an arrest warrant. It's my boss who's come to fire me in person. It's a reporter ready to do a story on the gynecologist turned sex worker, though they've got their time line backward.

Still, any of those might've been less shocking than June standing on our small stoop, a man dressed in a black suit behind her.

I open the door and she steps inside without an invitation, the toe of her stiletto clipping my shoe. As she walks, the man follows her. He's obviously a security guard of some sort.

Either that or a hit man.

My throat goes dry.

"June?" Willa's voice breaks through the room. She storms toward us but stops just shy of reaching me. "What are you doing in my house?"

I suspect she's trying to sound threatening, though, in reality, it comes across as terrified. When I spot her, she's staring at the man behind June in horror.

"What? You guys are allowed to come to my house anytime you want, but I'm not allowed to come to yours?" She practically cackles, obviously pleased with herself.

"What do you mean?" Willa asks. This time, she's looking at me.

"I was—"

I start to answer, but June interrupts. "Uh-oh. Trouble in paradise? He didn't tell you he came to my house today?"

"No, there is no trouble," I say firmly. "I was planning

to tell her. You just interrupted."

Willa moves next to me and takes my hand. "What do you want, June?"

The woman narrows her eyes at my wife. "I wanted to tell you in person that I will not be hounded by the two of you any longer. Today was a disaster. Drop-ins and unexpected meetings are unacceptable. I have tried to be nice and accommodating, but this"—she jabs a finger through the air toward the ground—"is where it ends."

"*Accommodating?*" Willa scoffs. "Are you kidding me? You think it's *accommodating* for you to ask us to kidnap a child for you?"

Unaffected, June continues. "From now on, the only time we will speak is when you have updates for me on the child. I will expect them weekly until the due date." She pauses. "When is it, by the way?"

I swallow.

"When is what?" Willa asks. Her hand wraps around my forearm, the other squeezing my hand tightly.

"The due date. Of the baby Mr. Ashley told me about this morning."

Heat creeps up my neck, and I feel the weight of Willa's stare, the way she loosens her grip on my hand slightly.

I clear my throat. "She's due in September."

June nods. "Great. Updates weekly until then." She counts on her fingers like she's forgetting something, then her eyes widen. She addresses Willa next. "Oh, right, and do not *ever* try to cross me again." Her voice is a low growl, her expression seething. She's so close to her they're almost touching. "Or these…" She points to the man behind her. When he reaches into his pocket, I flinch and move in front of Willa, separating her from whatever is coming. Her phone chimes from inside the pocket of her jeans. "Will go straight to the police."

I turn as Willa pulls out her phone. I don't need to look at the screen to know they're the pictures from the hotel, the ones that paint me as a monster.

Willa surprises me by keeping her face steady. Whatever reaction June is hoping for, my wife isn't giving it to her.

"Do you understand?" June demands, speaking to her as if Willa is a toddler and she's her disappointed parent.

"We understand," I answer for her, turning back to June.

"I want to hear her say it." She sidesteps and points a wrinkled finger at my wife. I have the urge to bite it off and spit it back into her face. Suddenly, the room feels too small. The air is too hot. Sweat gathers at the nape of my neck, bile rising in my throat.

This woman needs to get out of my house.

Willa locks her phone screen and slides the device into her back pocket, her gaze steely, lips tight. "I understand."

"Good. You will get me a child. An infant. No more problems. No more fighting. Once you do, your secrets will be safe."

She turns to walk away but freezes, looking back at Willa with a menacing grin. "Mr. Ashley isn't the only one with secrets, after all. Is he?"

# CHAPTER EIGHTEEN

### WILLA

When the door shuts, Hudson turns to me. I feel as if I'm standing naked in a crowd. My cheeks burn with heat and confusion.

"What was she talking about?" Hudson asks.

"I could ask you the same thing." I stare at him in disbelief. I only know of one baby due in September. "What baby is she talking about?"

The color drains from his face. "I... Okay, look, it's not great. I told her about Murphy. It was just to buy us time."

*No.*

*No.*

*No.*

"*What?* Why would you do that? Do you understand what you just did?" I throw my hands out to the sides, folding them into clenched fists. I'm so angry I could combust.

"I wasn't planning to tell her. I went to her house this

morning because I was trying to get a feel for how she spends her day, what's important to her. After our talk this morning, I just felt so helpless. I wanted to take back some of our power, catch her by surprise. I was going to try and find a way to stop this somehow. But she caught me and she was threatening you, and it just... I just blurted it out."

"So, what? You sacrificed Murphy to save me?"

"What? No, I—"

"You are my husband, Hudson, but she is my best friend. You cannot, *you will not*, hurt her to help me. Do you understand? I will forgive you for a lot of things, but I will never forgive you for that."

"I would never hurt her!" he shouts. "You know that."

I can't breathe. Can't think. "Then why would you do this? She hasn't even decided that she wants to put the baby up for adoption. She was just talking to me. Venting, really."

"I know that. Look, you're the one who brought it up. I would never have mentioned it if you hadn't."

My chest swells with rage, and he must see the explosion coming because he quickly heads it off with, "And I'm not saying it's your fault. Of course it's not. I will fix this, okay? It slipped out. I was just trying to think on my feet."

I puff out a breath, jabbing my fingers into the space between my eyes. "You're right. I brought it up first. I did. But it was only to see what you thought. I wasn't saying I could do it. I was just... God, I was just talking to you, Hudson. To my husband. Not to my *kidnapping co-*

*conspirator*! I was just trying to talk through one of the worst possible things I've ever considered doing. You had to know I wasn't serious. You had to know how much this would kill me. I can't believe you would use that in a conversation with that woman without even talking to me about it first. We are in this together. These are decisions we have to make together." I pound a hand against my chest, begging him to see how much this hurts me.

What have I done?

What have I done to my best friend?

This can't be happening.

What kind of monster am I?

"I understand that. I do. It wasn't a decision. I wasn't making a decision. It was a slip. Just a slip." He puts his hands on my arms, locking eyes with me. "But a slip that has bought us extra time. June agreed to wait months in exchange for updates. That's a good thing, right? We have more time."

I back out of his embrace, massaging either side of my nose with one hand. "Sure. It's a good thing if you have a plan to get us out of this. Do you?"

His silence is enough of an answer.

"I didn't think so. What are you going to do if she decides to keep it? Are we going to kidnap our godson? Really? Is that what this has come to?"

I'm being dramatic now, I know. Hudson would never. But I'm so angry. So, so angry at him. Like I've never been before.

We don't know how to have these kinds of arguments. It's so unlike us, but I can't calm myself down. Hopelessness has begun to take over and rage is the only thing that quiets it.

As if he's reading my mind, Hudson lowers his voice. "Honey, please. You know me. This is not us. We don't fight like this. Please don't let her get between us. It's what she wants."

I'm silent. Still waiting for my answer. "You didn't answer the question."

"Of course we're not going to kidnap Murphy's baby. I didn't know it required an answer. My god. I'm not a monster. The way you're looking at me... You'd think you didn't know me at all."

"Maybe I don't."

He rakes a hand through his hair, actively trying to keep himself calm. I can see it, and yet, I can't help. I want him to get angry with me. I deserve it after what I've done. How could I bring Murphy into this? All I've ever done is try to protect her.

"And do I know you?" he asks finally.

"What the hell does that mean?"

"What was all that stuff about me not being the only one with secrets? What was she talking about?"

"Nothing," I say quickly. Too quickly. "I don't know. I've told you everything. I don't have any secrets."

Only one. And it's one there's no way June knows, so it's irrelevant. She was just trying to scare us. To make us do exactly what we're doing.

"She's just trying to make us not trust each other," I say, my heart rate slowing finally. I can catch my breath again, the realization coming as quickly as the rage had.

"Never going to happen." Hudson steps forward, wrapping me in his arms. Just like that, the fight is over. "We have worked too hard to ever let her get between what we've built. We're strong. We can get through this." He lifts my chin so my eyes meet his. "We can, can't we?"

He's right, of course. We're stronger than whatever she throws our way. I just have to remember that. I can't let her make me forget.

"What are we going to do, Hudson?"

He drops his head. His brows knit together as if he's thinking hard. "We could hire a hit man."

My chest tightens. "What?"

"I'm only joking, I guess. It was just a thought. When she came in with that man, I thought he was..."

"You thought he was here to kill us?"

His lips press into a thin line, and he nods.

"We couldn't," I say softly. "We aren't killers."

"I know." His hand lifts to my face, and he rubs a thumb across my cheek.

"We aren't like her. We don't hurt people."

He kisses my forehead. "I would hurt someone to protect you."

I know it's true, and the sincerity with which he says it terrifies me. I can't let this happen. I can't let him lose himself over this woman's ridiculous mission. "I think we should hire a private investigator," I say eventually.

His brows draw down. "A private investigator to look into June?"

"Yes. Someone who could be discreet. Follow her around. Find out who she is and how she knows so much about us." The more I talk about it, the more convinced I am that this is the right answer. Our only option.

Hudson doesn't look as certain. "You heard her, though. No crossing her. I mean, I have no idea how she knew I was outside her house or how she got out of her house and to my car without me seeing her, but she did. She's protected, Willa. Whatever we do, we have to be careful."

"Exactly. Which is why a private investigator is so smart. We can make it look as if we're just going about our day-to-day life, as if we're letting it go and moving on with getting her this baby. All the while, we have five months to get as much dirt on her as possible." I pat his chest. "Come on. It might be our only chance at ending this once and for all."

He twists his lips, thinking. "Alright," he says, finally.

"Yeah?"

"Yeah." He kisses me. "Let's do it."

# CHAPTER NINETEEN

## HUDSON

"So, how exactly does this work?" Willa asks.

The man sitting across from us is named Mike. He has a thick head of dark, graying hair and a five-o'clock shadow that tells us of his long hours. Four empty paper coffee cups rest on his desk, each of them varying degrees of crushed, next to the one he's drinking from.

It's been a little over a week since Willa suggested finding a private investigator, and apparently, this rather frazzled-looking gentleman is our best hope.

He grumbles and downs the remaining liquid from the paper coffee cup, crushing it in his palm and adding it to the growing pile.

The trash can next to his desk is overflowing with fast-food bags and more crushed paper cups.

This guy is living on caffeine and a dream.

He wipes a wrinkled hand over his mouth, clearing his throat.

"I'll dig into the subject's past. Her history.

Marriages. Employment. Childhood. Her credit. Any criminal history. All known associates. I'll look for any connections between the three of you besides the obvious. I'll also put a tail on her, see her comings and goings. We'll change up vehicles and schedules every day so she doesn't suspect a thing. I want to know where she's spending her time. What's important to her. *Who's* important to her. Basically, anything there is to know about her, I'll find out."

He nudges a stack of papers across his desk to clear space for him to make notes. "I'll bill you by the hour. You can set a cap if you need to or let me work as much as is necessary. Up to you."

"And how quickly do you think you can have all of that to us?" Willa asks. "All of the answers?"

"If I work on it nonstop? A week or two, most likely. Maybe a month. I'll send you updates as I come across new information, so when we've found something useful, we can stop then. But I'll keep going and keep digging as long as you authorize me to. Until you've found what it is you're looking for."

"And you're sure she won't know about it? This woman, Ms. Cromwell, she's powerful. She has unlimited resources and seems to have eyes everywhere."

He gives her a patronizing grin that settles in my stomach like curdled milk. "Sweetheart, if I wasn't discreet, I wouldn't still be in business. You have nothing to worry about."

Willa looks at me, though she's already made up her mind. Mike has the personality of the soggy Taco Bell wrapper rotting on his floor, but we've heard he's the best. I nod.

"We want you to start right away. Find anything and everything you can about her," Willa says.

"*That* I can do." The man holds out a hand to me with a smile, but it's Willa who takes it.

*Misogynistic asshole.*

I offer a small grin and stand, shaking his hand next. I follow my wife out of the room and out of the office. We make it to our cars in silence.

"This will be good," she assures me. "He will help us."

I nod. I'm not totally sure I agree, but I do think it's our best chance moving forward. "Fingers crossed." My response is halfhearted at best, my optimism waning. "I gotta get to work. See you tonight."

I ease into my car but wait and watch for her to do the same and drive away safely before I leave.

---

As I near the end of the day, I'm exhausted. My feet hurt, my back hurts, my brain hurts.

Before, on days like this, I would order takeout and we'd have an easy night on the couch. Since meeting June, none of our nights have been easy. We've taken turns spiraling, waiting for the worst to happen.

Last night, it was Willa again, who spent half the night looking up what life is like in prison and pricing flights out of the country.

A few nights ago, I located our passports and wrote a letter to her that I hid inside a book she loves, just in case.

We're starting to lose it. Us. Our marriage. Our sanity. I'm not sure how much more of this we can take. Murphy still hasn't decided on whether to put the baby up for adoption, and we can't bring ourselves to decide what we'd do either way.

"Last patient is new," Kyla, one of the nurses, tells me as I head for the exam room.

I grab the iPad from the nurses' station and open the waiting chart. I read through it as I make my way down the hall to the patient's room, though when I open the door, it's not *Cecilia Burke, age fifty-five*, waiting for me, but rather *June Cromwell, batshit crazy.*

The photo on the patient's file doesn't look a thing like June. In fact, I'm pretty sure it's a stock photo.

*How is it possible no one caught this?*

Too shocked to be angry with the nurses and front desk staff, I shut the door behind me in a hurry. It takes everything in my power not to lunge across the room at her. Maybe it's only the fact that there are nurses, doctors, and other patients right down the hall that stops me.

"What the hell are you doing here, June?"

She turns around on the examination table, the white paper underneath her crackling loudly with the movement. "Don't you mean *Cecilia?*"

"No, I *don't* mean Cecilia. Why are you here? *How* are you here?" I lower my voice, wagging the iPad in my hand toward her. "Insurance fraud is a serious crime, do you know that?"

She gasps, covering her mouth. "Why, I'd hate to be a criminal. Tell me, what's that like?"

This is all a game to her.

"*Shut up!*" I demand, trying my hardest to keep my voice low. The walls are paper thin here. "Please. You have to leave. You cannot be at my place of work. You have to go. *Now.*"

"Oh, I understand. Don't worry. I'm not here for an exam. I just needed to deliver something to you in a place where I knew I couldn't be set up." She climbs from the table and crosses the room to the chair where her purse is resting, pulling out two slips of paper.

"What are you talking about? What's this?"

"End it. Now." I'm still processing what she's said as she passes the papers to me. When I flip them over, I realize they're not papers at all. Instead, I find myself staring at two photographs.

Of us.

Leaving the private investigator's office.

"How do you—"

"End it," she repeats. "I already warned you about what would happen if you crossed me."

"You had us followed."

She nods. "I'm protecting my investment. I knew you two wouldn't give up so easily. I admire that, actually, but it's time to stop. Stop fighting me and let's work together."

"Fine. Sure." I just need her out of here.

"That simple, hmm?"

"Yes, you win, June." I drop the pictures down to my side, refusing to look at them.

"We'll see." She gives me a dubious look.

"Now, will you please go?"

She sighs. "Soon enough. Unfortunately, I have one small piece of business to take care of before I do."

Ice sinks in my core.

"What's that?"

"Well, Mr. Ashley, as I've told you, I am nothing if not a woman of my word. I gave you my word there would be consequences the next time you tried to find a way out of this."

The ice spreads, settles in my chest, and squeezes my lungs. "You don't need to do anything. I hear you loud and clear, okay? We'll call him off, June. It's fine. We didn't even hire him. It was just a meeting. We're trying to protect ourselves—"

"I understand." She waves off my sentence, ending it before I'm done. "Truly, I do. But unfortunately, as a soon-to-be mother, I understand that if I let this slide, there will be another time. And another. And another. Spare the rod, spoil the child, and all that."

I steel myself. "What are you going to do?"

"Oh, relax, nothing so bad this time. Just a small punishment to that wife of yours."

Every hair on my body seems to stand on end. "No. Leave Willa out of this."

"You mean to tell me the private investigator wasn't her idea?"

"Yes." I lie without hesitation. "She didn't even want to meet with him. It was all me."

She gives a dry laugh and pats me on the chest. "Nice try, but you see, I'm afraid I just don't believe you."

Images of a bleeding Willa flash through my mind. I swallow them down, refusing to think such things. "If you hurt her, this is all over. I won't help you. I won't do anything for you. She is off-limits, June. Do you hear me? Without her, this all goes away."

"I'm not going to hurt her. Not yet, anyway. Think of this as a... What do they call them? A yellow card? I'm still learning these child-rearing terms. It's barely more than a warning. Enough to let you both know just how seriously I'm taking all of this."

"What are you going to do?"

Her lips curl into a cruel smile. "I'm going to reveal her secret. I thought I'd given her enough of a hint, but apparently, she needs me to spell it out. I'm going to share with her what I know and exactly how serious I am about bringing you both down if you try to cross me. If it happens again, I won't hesitate to send you both to jail."

"Jail? Both of us?" I'm dizzy. Teeming with rage.

"Yes. I want your wife to know what I am capable of if either of you acts out against me again."

"She's done nothing wrong. Whatever you think you have on her, she's no criminal."

The smile falls from her face, and she narrows her eyes at me. "Whatever I *think* I have..." Her voice quiets. "Wait a second. Oh, this is good. This is good, Mr. Ashley." She waves a finger at me as if she's hit the jackpot. I'm still clueless as to what's happening. When she lowers her hand, she's still watching me, as if we're playing a game I've not been taught the rules to.

"What is happening right now?"

She crosses her arms and cocks a hip, her head shaking slowly from side to side. "You... You have no idea what she did, do you?"

# CHAPTER TWENTY

### WILLA

Before I leave the office, Murphy texts me a picture of the flowers I had delivered to her apartment. Some of them are more wilted than I would've liked, but she seems happy enough.

I have no idea what I'm supposed to be doing to support my friend, but I'm trying my hardest to let her know I'm here should she need anything. That I'm always thinking of her.

She still hasn't said anything else about her decision and I'm trying to give her time, but I'm growing more anxious about her inaction by the minute.

When I arrive home, Hudson's car is already in the driveway. Palpable fear settles in me, sticking to my shallow breath like frost on a cold day, but I try to shove it down. Ignore it. This doesn't mean anything's wrong. Maybe he got off early. Maybe he left because he was sick.

Even as I make my way in the door, I know I'm lying to myself.

Hudson never leaves work early without a good reason, and if he were sick, he would've called me.

"Hud?" I call into the quiet house. "You home?"

When he doesn't answer, I drop my keys in the bowl, place my purse and jacket on the entry table, and cross through the living room on my way to the kitchen.

A light in the hallway stops me in my tracks. I turn my attention to it, realizing he's in the office.

"Hudson?" I call again. "You there?"

"In here." His tone is flat, but he's alive. Not in prison. I can work with that.

I suck in a shallow breath and make my way down the hall and to the office. When I stick my head inside with a small smile, I hope and pray he'll return it.

He doesn't.

"Everything okay?"

He's sitting at our desk, staring at the computer monitor with a solemn expression. When his eyes flick up to me, he rests his hands in front of him, his face as blank as if we were having a business meeting.

I don't understand what's happening.

"June knows we tried to hire a private investigator. We have to fire Mike. Tell him to stop whatever he's doing."

Ice sluices through my veins, and I step farther into the room. "What? No. We can't. How does she know? How do you know she knows?"

"She came to visit me at work. Pretended she was a patient."

"What? How can she do that?"

He looks as exasperated as I feel. The dark circles around his eyes are worse than they were yesterday—much worse than a week ago. "Jesus Christ, I don't know. Maybe she paid off a nurse. Maybe she got a fake ID. For all I know, she knocked a patient out and shoved her in a broom closet. What I do know is that she knows. She has pictures of us leaving his office."

I need to sit down. I don't feel so well.

"She said we have to end it before things get worse."

"But we've already paid him for the first ten hours of work."

He shrugs. "I don't think she cares, Willa. Fire him. What choice do we have?"

I ease into the chair across from him, staring into space with confusion. "She had us followed?"

"She's *having* us followed. Actively. Yes. Probably will continue to do so until we hand her a no-strings-attached infant."

"Okay, but the investigator isn't *us*. We'll never see him in person again. How could she possibly know whether or not we fire him?"

"Do you honestly think she won't have him followed, too? She's expecting him to be watching her now. Whatever he was planning to do, it's over."

I nod, dropping my chin to my chest. Defeat weighs heavily on me. It's not enough that we already had very limited options. Now it feels like we have absolutely none. I have the sudden urge to close all the curtains, turn off all the lights. For all we know, she's hacked into all our devices. She could be listening to this conversation in real time.

"Well, what did you tell her?"

"I told her we'd call him off. That it was just a meeting anyway and we hadn't hired him. I told her it was my idea."

A bloom of appreciation grows in my chest. "Thank you."

"But she had to punish us for breaking her rules. She's a *woman of her word*, after all." His words drip with venom.

Chills line my arms. "What do you mean? Punish us, how?"

He gives me a slow nod as if confirming something I don't understand. "She told me your secret. She was planning to confirm it to you to prove how dangerous she is, but when she realized I had no idea, I guess she decided this was better."

"Secret?" My brows draw together. I can't breathe. Can't think.

Because there is only one secret I've never told my husband. And it's impossible for him to know it.

His face breaks. Withers. Wrinkles with such devastation, it kills me. "Tell me it isn't true."

I ball my hands into fists.

*I will kill her.*

*I will kill her.*

*I will kill her.*

136

"What did she tell you, Hudson?"

Not this. Anything but this. He will never look at me the same. I will forever be flawed in his eyes after this. Merely human. A monster.

"She told me about the fire."

The words are all he has to say for me to know what he knows. To know it's all over.

It's as if I've been doused with scalding water. My body screams, radiating heat. My thoughts come out jumbled.

"H-How could she know about that? No one knows about that."

A muscle in his cheek twitches. "So it's true?"

"I... I'm so sorry." I force the words out, licking my lips as I try to focus. It's impossible. "I don't know what to say."

"Say anything," he begs, his hands folded together in front of him on the desk, fingers intertwined. "Something. Help me understand what happened."

"Hudson, I was so young. I never meant for..." There's nothing I could ever say to make this okay, so I give up trying. There's just one thing I need to understand. Only one thing I can focus on. "How could she possibly know about that night?"

"*She knows everything!*" he shouts, his clasped hands breaking apart before he pounds his fists on the desk. My beautiful, brilliant husband is falling to pieces right in front of me. She's ruined him. Destroyed everything. "Including this." He presses his lips together. Looks away. "I didn't even know this."

"You don't understand. No one does. No one knows. It's not as if it's something I'm proud of. I hate myself for what I did. It was the worst night of my life."

His skin is practically gray. Lifeless. "Why wouldn't you tell me? You know everything about me. Everything, Willa. I thought we were partners. Friends first, that's always been the deal. I thought you trusted me."

"It's not about trust." I lean forward, reaching for his hands. To my relief, he doesn't pull away. His palms are freezing under mine. "It's not. I swear to you. It's about being mortified over that night. Never wanting to talk about it again. Never wanting you to judge me for what I did. Please don't hate me for this. I couldn't stand it."

"What happened? Why did you do it?"

"I can't..." My throat is tight with rage and fear. "Please don't make me do this. I can't talk about that night. Not yet."

He opens his mouth, prepared to argue, but I cut him off.

"When I'm ready, I swear I'll tell you everything."

"Willa, I need to know. I'm involved in this now."

"You will. You will know, I swear it. Just give me time. I..." I meet his eyes as mine swim with tears. "Please, just give me time to process. I never wanted to talk about that night again."

He shakes his head and pulls his hands back. "I don't hate you. But I do hate being blindsided. I won't let this go. Eventually, you'll have to tell me."

"I will."

He stares down at his hands, folding and unfolding

them. Eventually, he says, "Is there anything else you haven't told me? Anything besides the fire?"

I shake my head, wiping away fresh tears as they fall down my cheeks. "No, nothing else. Of course there's nothing else. I'm so sorry you found out this way. I don't understand how she could possibly know about the fire."

He turns the desktop monitor around to face me so I can see what he's been looking at. The headline burns me to this day.

I can still smell the smoke. Taste it, even.

My eyes sting just thinking about it.

"I don't know, Willa. But she does."

## Nine Teens Killed in Fire During Unsupervised House Party. Police Suspect Arson.

# CHAPTER TWENTY-ONE

## HUDSON

I can't bear to look Murphy in the eyes, so it's a good thing my attention is focused elsewhere for the majority of her exam.

I run the Doppler over her lower stomach, grinning when I locate the heartbeat.

"One hundred fifty-two. Healthy as a horse."

She stares at the ceiling with a blank face, holding her shirt up with a viselike grip. I lower the Doppler and reach for her shirt, pulling it back in place gently. The movement seems to break her out of a trance, and she looks down at me. I can tell there's something she wants to say, but she's holding back.

"So, is there anything you want to talk about? Any issues or concerns? You can sit up." I back away and take a seat on the rolling stool. I'm doing all I can to be professional with her, but it's hard to see her as a patient when she's the closest thing I have to a sister-in-law as well as a potential ticket to freedom from the mess my life has become.

I really hate myself right now.

She does as I've said, sitting up on the table with her hands propped behind her. She stares at the poster on the wall detailing the many birth control options we offer.

"I'm still having morning sickness. My old doctor said it would end by now, but it hasn't."

I pull up her chart and type in a note. "Usually, it does lighten up around fourteen weeks, so he was right. Ideally, you should be well past it at this point, but it's not uncommon for it to last a little while longer or even the entire pregnancy in some cases. I'd like to run a few tests just to make sure everything looks okay."

"You think something's wrong?" she asks with wide eyes.

"I'm sure everything's fine. But I like to err on the side of caution. In the meantime, we can prescribe you some medicine to help alleviate the morning sickness. You'll take it at night before bed, and it should resolve the nausea pretty quickly."

"Thanks." She scoots forward, dangling her legs off the end of the table, swinging them back and forth.

"You're measuring right on track, though. Everything seems perfectly normal. No protein in your urine. Blood pressure's great. Heartbeat's healthy. Do you feel like you've been able to keep enough food down?"

"I'm basically living on crackers right now." She looks at me with a new flicker of worry in her eyes. "Is that bad?"

"Well, we want to have a well-rounded diet for proper fetal development, but whatever you're able to keep down is better than nothing. You're taking a prenatal vitamin, right?"

She nods.

"Great. That'll help fill in the gaps, too."

"Okay, cool."

I wait, trying to give her space to say anything else she might want to. With any other patient, I'd be standing by now, preparing to leave the room.

When she doesn't say anything for a long while, I prompt her, "Any other concerns? Any pain? Bleeding?"

"No. Not really."

"Good. That's good. We'll"—I check her chart—"uh, we'll do an anatomy scan at your next appointment, where we can look over everything to make sure the baby is still on track and measuring where they should. You'll be able to learn the sex at that point if you want."

She's quiet for a moment, staring down at her hands in her lap.

"It's up to you," I add. "Some people prefer not to know."

The words seem to trigger something in her. "She told you I'm considering adoption."

I'm not sure it's a question, but I nod anyway. "She did."

"And? What do you think?"

"I think..." I ease my stool closer to her. "I think you'd be an excellent mom, Murphy. If that's what you want to do. You're not an addict. You have your own place. You've always kept a job."

"Wow, I mean, I should basically run for president with a résumé like that, shouldn't I?"

I return her sarcastic look, used to her using humor to override her stress. "I'm not saying it would be easy. It would require a lot of patience and there would be a lot to learn. But you're smart. And patient. You've always been there for Willa when she needs you. If you want to do this, you can. And we'll be here for you every step of the way. But if you don't want to do this, if you choose to give the baby up for adoption, it won't be because you don't care."

She looks up at me with a pained expression as tears well in her eyes. "I don't want this baby to think I didn't love them."

"They won't." I'm up without thought, an awkward hand on her shoulder. I want to pull it away instantly, but I resist the urge. "Adoption is one of the most selfless things you can do for your child if you don't feel ready or equipped to raise it. No one could judge you for that. Willa will help you find the baby an amazing home."

She swipes away a tear, groaning loudly. "Is there anything you can do about these damn hormones? I cried over a podcast ad the other day."

"I'm afraid there's nothing I can do about that," I tell her with a chuckle. "It just means your body is doing what it's supposed to."

She sniffles, shoving me playfully. "Well, what good are you, then?"

"Not much. Then again, you chose me, so what does that say about your judgment?"

She laughs, and I'm so relieved I've made it happen. The awkwardness from earlier, the guilt, has evaporated. At least for the moment. "Fair point." She eyes me. "You had shitty parents, didn't you?"

Always blunt, this one.

I nod. She knows I did.

I lock the iPad's screen, stepping back. "For a short while, anyway. They were addicts. We were homeless most of my childhood. Bouncing around from one place to the next, staying with this friend and that." Crossing the room, I push the stool back under the counter. "I don't remember either of them ever being clean. Ever playing with me. Nothing like that. Then again, I don't have a lot of memories from that time anyway. My mom overdosed when I was eight. Dad died by suicide two weeks later."

When I turn back around, she's studying me silently.

"This isn't the kind of conversation I usually have in these rooms," I tell her with an embarrassed frown.

"You were in foster care after that."

Again, I nod.

She sighs, kicking her feet so hard her heels bang into the metal underside of the examination table. "My parents sucked too. Well, my dad was never around. He'd show up occasionally when I was little, looking for a place to crash, promising he'd stick around, but it never lasted. My mom was just burned out. She worked three jobs most of my life, and in her rare time off, she didn't have time for a kid. I raised myself for the most part." There's a long pause. Then she adds, "I have no idea how to be a parent. I was never shown how."

"I think these things are kind of just instinct."

"What if it's not, though? What if the baby gets here and I have no idea what to do with it? What if I don't like it? What if it doesn't like me? I really don't want to screw this kid up."

"Those are all valid concerns."

"Now you're back to being my doctor, hmm?"

I cross my arms, leaning against the wall behind me. "Look, it's scary, I get it. Having bad parents messes you up. There's no denying that."

"Which is why you guys don't have kids. You don't think you'd be any good at it." Again, she's asking a question without really asking, though I suspect Willa has already answered this for her.

"That's not the only reason."

She rolls her eyes.

"It's not," I insist. "We just aren't in a place to have kids. Neither of us is sure we want them, and even if we do later on, now's not the time for us. I think a lot of people have kids before they've thought about what they want. It's a big decision."

"Well, if *you guys* aren't ready, *I'm* definitely not."

"Fair, but a lot of people weren't ready and they still turned out to be great parents."

"Yeah? Name one."

"Uh, well, a lot of my patients," I bullshit her, though I suspect she's not buying it. "So, I can't name any, but there are hundreds. Thousands, maybe. Just, you know, privacy laws and everything." I grin.

"You're a bad liar, Hudson."

If she only knew how well I lie for a living.

I clear my throat. "You'll be fine, Murphy. If this is what you want, you'll be fine. This baby will be lucky to have you."

She looks as if she's on the verge of tears again when she asks, "If you were me, what would you do?"

Guilt bites at my organs, varying responses swarming through my head. There's one right answer and one answer that has the potential to save my life. My marriage.

This isn't about me. It's about her.

Murphy is not the answer to my problems. She can't be.

"I have no idea, to be honest. It's not an easy decision. But I think you'll make the right one, whatever you decide."

"That's not an answer, doc."

"I can't make your decision for you, Murphy. No one can. It's yours and yours alone to make." She deflates, so I add, "But, for what it's worth, I don't think you can make a wrong choice here."

She frowns, then goes quiet. After what feels like a long time, I push off from the wall. "If there's nothing else you need to talk about, I'll go out and get a nurse to bring you back for some blood work. Then I'll get this prescription called in to your pharmacy for you to pick up today."

I reach for the door handle, but she stops me in my tracks. "Hudson, wait."

I turn back. "Yeah?"

"Is it okay? Me being here?"

"Of course." I force myself to smile at her, not sure if it's a lie.

"I know it's weird, after everything. I just... Thank you, I guess. For this."

I reach for the door handle, desperate to escape this conversation, which is entering into dangerous territory. "We're going to get through this, Murphy. *You're* going to get through this. I'm happy to help however I can."

Before I can open the door, I hear her voice again. "Do you feel guilty?" she asks.

I swallow without looking at her. I can't bear to. "Every single day."

With that, I pull the door open and step out into the hall.

*Every single day.*

# CHAPTER TWENTY-TWO

## WILLA

> How are you? How did the appointment go?

I text Murphy to quiet my racing thoughts, but it's not doing any good.

I'm losing my mind.

I've become consumed with thoughts of June and worries about what's going to happen next. Hidden danger seems to be lurking around every corner. Things that can, and likely will, go wrong.

I don't understand how she could know about the fire when I've spent my life hiding from it, making sure there is nothing to connect me to that night. Even if June had hired an investigator of her own, there would be nothing to lead her to me.

Unless I've missed something.

What could I have missed?

I don't understand how we got here or why things

have become so disastrous so fast. I do understand there are people out there who won't like what we do, who judge Hudson, and who probably judge me even more harshly. As a woman, it is probably all my fault in someone's mind. Regardless, even if you find our lifestyle and the way we've chosen to claw our way out of debt abhorrent, I hope we can at least agree on the fact that we've done nothing wrong. Illegal doesn't always equal immoral. We are good people. Decent people. People who are just trying to build a life for ourselves, better than the lives we had as children.

And now, our lives are being threatened. My husband's career, which he's worked tirelessly for, sacrificed so much for, is being threatened. Our freedom is hanging by a thread, controlled by one selfish, single-minded woman.

The fire, one could argue, was both immoral and illegal. But it's the past. A terrible, terrible mistake. One I've paid for with immeasurable guilt every day since that night.

June has no right to do this, though I can see no way through.

I'm combing through her file again when my office door pops open and Starla sticks her head inside. She's already told me once today that I seem out of it. I blamed it on being under the weather, but I'm still expecting her to say something about my performance lately, or rather, a lack thereof. Instead, she gives me a smile and places a box on my desk.

"What's this?"

"A package came for you at reception."

I stand, reading over the label, but there's no return address. Just a printed paper with my name and the office address on it.

My heart pounds in my chest so hard I think I may be sick.

"Okay. Thanks, Starla."

"Sure thing, doll."

She backs out of the office as I study the box, trying to decide what to do. There's no indication of who it's from. For all I know, it could be a thank-you present from one of our clients, but deep down, I know. I know whatever is in this box won't be good.

I run through the options: photographs, a human head, an animal head, a clump of hair, something from my house, something from the fire.

I swallow and grab the scissors from my drawer, slicing through the tape and unfolding each flap of the box in a hurry. With shaking hands, I pull back the final flap and stare down into the box's depths.

A bit anticlimactic.

Inside is a small, silver handheld tape recorder with a note taped over the speaker.

*Press play.*

I pull it out, turning it over in my hands. It's heavier than I expected. It's been years since I've seen anything like this. I vaguely remember having a similar one as a child that I'd hide around my house, trying to record something interesting after reading *Harriet the Spy*.

I never managed to catch anything, though. To be sure, I suffered through hours and hours of our family moving through the house; my cat, Percy, purring loudly into the microphone; and, once, a neighbor stopping by to drop off a piece of mail that arrived in his mailbox.

Nothing spy-worthy.

I don't know where that recorder ever ended up.

Holding this recorder in my hand with the command to listen to whatever secrets it holds taunting me, I'm torn between fear and curiosity.

In the end, curiosity wins out. I press the button and hold my breath.

For a second, there is only silence, then the whirring of the tape and an occasional crackle or pop of the device.

I half expect to hear Jigsaw ask if I want to play a game.

Then I hear her voice. Chills crawl up the back of my neck.

"It's wrong. I know it is. I'm not an evil person. But I can't stop myself."

"Why do you think you let it continue if you feel so strongly that it's wrong?" a man's voice asks. She's talking to someone I don't recognize.

There's a long pause. So long that I check the tape to be sure it's still playing.

"I don't know." I press my ear to the speaker again, not wanting to miss a thing. It sounds like she's crying.

"I think you do know, Murphy. You must."

"Because I care about him, I guess. He's fun. He gets me. Looks out for me."

"Everything you're describing, all of those things, can generally make for a healthy relationship. So, what makes this one wrong?"

"Everything."

"You're going to have to be more specific."

I hold my breath, not wanting anything to interrupt whatever this is. It feels intimate. Private. I shouldn't be listening.

"You know why."

"I know what you've told me in the past. I need to hear you say it."

"It's wrong because... Because he's not mine. Not really. He'll never leave her."

"His wife?" the man confirms. "Do you mean he'll never leave his wife, Murphy?"

She sobs, and I know her answer before she gives it.

"Yes."

The tape ends.

# CHAPTER TWENTY-THREE

## HUDSON

When I get home, I smell chicken pesto roasting in the oven. It feels like the first normal evening in so long, and gosh, how I've missed the normal. The boring, even.

I kick off my shoes and strip out of my jacket before making my way into the kitchen, where I find Willa waiting at the table. She places her phone face down when she sees me.

"Hey, honey."

"Come sit." She pats the table without saying hello.

I swallow. That tone of voice has never ended well for me.

"I feel like I'm in the principal's office. What did I do?" I make my way to the table and ease into my usual chair.

"I don't know, Hudson. Why don't you tell me?"

"Did Murphy say something to you?"

Her jaw goes tight. "Why would you assume that?"

"Well, I'm not sure what she said or what I did, but

I'm sure it's a misunderstanding. Things got kind of weird in her appointment today, and maybe I overshared—"

"Overshared? Is that what you want to call it? Really?" She scoffs, looking downright furious. "Apparently it's me who's been *sharing*, isn't it?"

Now I'm at a loss. "What do you mean?"

"How long has it been going on?" she demands.

"I'm... Wait, I'm confused. What are we talking about?"

"You and Murphy, Hudson. Don't play dumb. The jig is up."

"The jig is... What the hell are you talking about? What has Murphy got to do with anything? Did I do something wrong in her appointment?"

"Oh, no. I'm sure you did *all* the right things."

Her smug smile sours my stomach.

"Sweetheart, you're going to have to fill in some blanks for me. I swear to you, I have no idea what you're talking about."

She looks away, scratching her eyebrow. "You guilt-tripped me over my secret. My secret from over *eleven years* ago—well before I'd ever met you. You made me feel so bad for keeping it from you, and here you've been keeping this from me all this time. To this day. She's my best friend. How could you do this? Were you just going to keep me in the dark forever? Never tell me about you two?"

"What about us?" My stomach sinks, bile rising in my throat.

"Is the baby yours, too?" She covers her own stomach, her skin paling. She looks as if she may pass out, although maybe that's me. I can't focus on what she's doing as my brain processes the words that have just left her mouth.

"Is the baby mine? *Murphy's?* You're talking about Murphy's baby?"

Is this actually happening?

She's quiet. Still.

She blinks, her otherwise perfect face marred with distrust.

"What the... Why would you *ever* ask me that? Of course it's not. How could it be?"

Does she know? How could she know?

She doesn't know. I refuse to believe it. To accept it. How is any of this possible? Why is she looking at me this way?

"You're having an affair with her. Stop lying to me. I can't stand it." Her nose wrinkles with disgust as tears glisten in her amber eyes.

It's not a question, but my body revolts against it. I stand, shaking my head, holding out my hands in protest. "An affair? Are you *kidding* me? How could you think that? Why would I be having an affair with Murphy? *How* would I? I love *you*, Willa, with my whole heart. She's like my little sister. I would never do that to you. Or to her, for that matter. Where is this coming from?"

"Then why did I get this recording of her saying she's sleeping with a married man?" she asks, the tears rolling down her cheeks. She tries to swipe them away as quickly as they fall, but the effort is futile.

I can't stand to see her cry. It devastates me in the way other people can't see animals die in movies. Rips my insides to shreds. Makes me feel physically weak.

Especially when I'm the one who's caused it.

"What recording? What are you talking about?"

She lifts a tape recorder from the seat next to her and places it on the table.

"Where did you get that?"

"It was delivered to my office today, addressed to me. There was no note to let me know who sent it." She presses play, and I hear Murphy's voice almost immediately. She's talking to a man whose voice I don't recognize. Telling him she's in a relationship with someone. A man. A *married* man.

The tape ends.

I stare at her, waiting for more. "Is that it?"

She nods.

I drop back down in my seat. "Willa, I don't know who she's talking about. Do you know how many married men there are in this city? Why would you assume she's talking about me?"

"Because..." It seems like it's the first time it's occurred to her she could be wrong. "Because why else won't she tell me who the baby's father is?"

"Maybe because she's embarrassed that he's married. Maybe because she doesn't know. Maybe because it's not really anyone's business but hers. It doesn't matter. I can't believe you'd actually accuse me of sleeping with her." I run both hands through my hair. "Forget me. I can't believe you'd accuse your *best friend* of sleeping with

156

your *husband*. I mean, why would either of us do that? Do you honestly believe I'd hurt you in that way? I said no secrets, and I meant it. I love you, Willa. Come on. You know me."

At least, I thought she did.

She bites her lip, sitting uncomfortably in her chair. She looks as if she wants to shrink down. Disappear. "Do you swear you aren't sleeping with her? Swear it on my life? On yours? If you're lying, Hudson, if you lie to me now and I find out about it later, there's no coming back from it. Don't make a lie worse with anoth—"

"I swear to you I'm not. I swear to you I haven't. I wouldn't. I am not that man. I love you. The thought of losing you destroys me, Willa. Don't you get that?"

She nods, though a bit begrudgingly, and I pull her into me, kissing her lips. My lungs expand with what feels like the first full breath I've taken since I entered the room.

"You scared me," I whisper, nuzzling my face into her neck.

"I was scared," she admits, hugging me back just as tightly.

I pull away, bracing my hands on either side of her arms. "Who do you think sent that tape? How would they have it?"

"It has to be June, doesn't it?" she asks. "Who else?"

"June? Maybe, I guess, but why? How does she know anything about Murphy?"

She presses her lips together as if it's obvious. "Blackmail. That's clearly how she gets anything done.

157

Whoever it is on the tape talking to her, a coworker, maybe? Or a therapist? She must've been blackmailing them to get the recording to make us fight even more."

"But how would she have known Murphy was sleeping with a married man?"

She closes her eyes, letting out a long exhale. "I don't know. The same way she knows about the fire, I guess. I'm starting to feel like she knows everything about us. We have to figure out the connection. It seems more personal than just her wanting a baby. Why is she targeting us?"

"We made ourselves easy targets. Both of us have access to children. If Constance mentioned that I'd helped the woman at the bar that night, maybe it gave June the idea I'd help her, too. If she'd looked into us, maybe she realized how perfect the plan was. And now, to keep us in line, she's obviously having us followed. Maybe she's having our friends followed, too. It would explain how she knows about Murphy. Whatever it is, she wants us to doubt each other. She told me your secret. Now she's telling you things that aren't true about me. Her long game is to get us to turn on each other. But it won't happen. It can't."

"You're right." She pats my cheek, her thumb caressing my cheekbone. "This is what she wants." She leans back in her chair. "I'm sorry about all this. God, what a mess. I've just been so upset. I'm not thinking clearly."

"No. Hey, it's okay. I don't blame you." I squeeze her

thigh gently. "She is very good at this game. She knows how to get under our skin."

"I know. I have to stop letting her. I hate what she's doing to me. I feel like I'm going crazy, you know?"

"You aren't," I tell her, lifting her chin so she meets my eyes. "*You aren't.* Do you hear me?"

"I'm just so ready for this to all be over."

"Speaking of, today was Murphy's appointment." A shadow passes over her expression. Just a flash, and then it's gone. She hasn't completely forgotten or forgiven me for my imaginary crime. "She mentioned that she's still considering adoption."

"Yeah, I know. I texted her. I'm trying not to push," she says.

"Right. I didn't either. But it seems like she's leaning that way. We didn't do an ultrasound this time, but we will when she comes back. I made up an update to send June, just some fake stats. It doesn't feel right giving her real ones."

"No worse than giving her a real baby," she says softly, picking at a piece of chapped skin on her bottom lip. I realize then how dry her skin looks. Dull. She's losing her vibrancy over this. She looks tired. I can't remember the last time I saw her eat a full meal.

This is killing her.

*I* am killing her with my inaction. With my inability to fix this, save her, somehow.

"What if we just ran away? Bought a boat and sailed off the coast."

"Do you have millions put away you haven't told me about?" she teases.

"Not millions, and nothing you don't know about, but we might be able to swing some cruise or flight tickets if nothing else."

She doesn't even consider it. "She's having us followed, Hud. She'd know if we tried to leave. She knows everything."

I reach for her hand, running my thumb over her knuckles. "Not everything."

Her brows lift with surprise.

"Not how much I'm willing to do to protect you."

# CHAPTER TWENTY-FOUR

## WILLA

I apprehensively knock on the front door of Murphy's apartment. The wooden maroon door is covered in small spider webs and dust, and there's a bag of garbage next to the faded welcome mat I picked out for her two years ago.

I hate that I haven't been here lately. I know how exhausted she's been. How much she has needed me. If I hadn't been so preoccupied, I'd have been able to help more.

When she opens the door, I realize she's been sleeping. I check my watch. It's after ten, but obviously still too early.

Something else I've failed at.

She nudges one of her white tank top straps back onto her shoulder, rubbing her slightly protruding belly with one hand as she stifles a yawn.

She checks the clock on the wall. "What are you doing here?"

"Sorry, I didn't mean to wake you. I thought you'd already be up."

A piece of her strawberry-blonde hair falls into her eyes, and she shoves it back into the mountain of a messy bun atop her head, poking it in place with one finger until it sticks. "I worked the closing shift last night, so I didn't get home until after two." As if to prove a point, she yawns again, then steps back to allow me inside her apartment.

I place my purse on the small table next to the door and pull out my phone. This feels like a terrible idea, but it's all I can think of. I need answers and Murphy may be the only one who can give them to me. "I'm sorry to wake you. I just... I need to ask you something."

"Okay. You couldn't text me? Is it serious or something?"

"I'm not sure, honestly." I pull up a photo of June from her file and turn the phone around to Murphy, holding my breath. "Do you recognize this woman?"

She studies the picture, taking my phone from me as she stares at it. "I feel like my answer should be yes, but not really. Is she a politician? Am I failing a test right now?"

"You've never seen her before?"

"I don't think so. Who is she?"

I lock my phone screen and lie. "A patient of Hudson's. She's weird, though. I'm trying to find out who she is."

"And you thought I might know?"

"I thought you might've seen her around. Or at the bar, maybe."

She doesn't look convinced. "She doesn't exactly look like someone I'd see in the bar." Her head tilts to the side. "Are you okay, Wills? Is something wrong?"

"No." I wave off her concern. "No. I'm fine. Forget I said anything." I tuck my phone in my back pocket, theory gone, as I take in the state of the place. Everywhere I look, I find new reasons to feel guilty. The apartment is messier than usual, with dishes piled up on the coffee table next to an empty pizza box, a *Friends* hoodie and a pair of socks resting on the small couch, and a stack of books on the floor.

I promised myself I would help her through this pregnancy, and now, as soon as she needs me most, I've all but disappeared.

"What can I help with?" I ask, already getting to work, gathering her dirty clothes from the couch. I find another pair of socks on the floor and a T-shirt on the end table. "You look exhausted."

She readjusts her hair again and tugs at the waist of her flannel pajama pants. "I'm fine, Wills." Crossing the small living room to the kitchen, she opens the fridge and pulls out a bottle of water. She holds it out. "Want one?"

"No, thanks."

She shrugs, takes a small sip herself before setting it on the counter, and reaches for the pile of clothes from my hands. "You don't have to do anything. It's just been a long week. I was going to clean up today. I don't go in until eight, so I have time."

"Have you talked to your bosses about working fewer hours? Or more during the day? With your pregnancy, they should really be willing to make exceptions."

"Tony would move me to days if I asked, but I won't. Nights equal more tips." She tosses the clothes onto the hallway floor in front of the accordion-style door that hides the washer and dryer. "Is everything okay? You seem like you're on a mission other than asking me if I know some random woman. What am I missing?"

"Nope. No mission. I'm just here to visit." I return to the living room and gather the trash and pizza box, carrying everything to the kitchen.

She rounds the island, heading me off before I can make it to the trash can. "Okay, stop. What's going on? Why are you cleaning my apartment at ten a.m. on a Saturday?" She takes the pizza box from me and places it on the counter. "Something is up. I know you well enough to know."

I sigh. She's right. She can read me like one of the books haphazardly thrown on the carpet across the room. I rest my hands on my hips. "Okay, you're right. I am here with a slight mission. Other than the woman. We, um, we need to talk."

"Oh, shit. Are you breaking up with me?" she teases.

"It's not you, it's me," I say back, more out of habit than anything. I want this to continue between us. I know that. I want to still be her best friend. To still love her as I always have.

"That's what they always say, you bitch." She bumps my hip with hers, then crosses the room and flops down on the couch sideways so she can face me, drawing her legs up under her. She eyes me expectantly, patting the couch cushion. "So, talk, sister. What's the *hot goss*?"

I sit down, adjusting to face her, too. I close my eyes, bracing myself for what's to come. "I need to know who the father of your baby is."

"What?" She laughs like I must be joking. I wish I was. "But... Why? Why does it matter? You don't know him. Is this for the adoption paperwork? He doesn't know about the baby. He won't be a problem. It was just a one-night stand. I told you."

I stare at her, waiting out the silence, waiting for her to say more.

"Why are you staring at me like I'm on my deathbed? Jesus Christ, what did Hudson say to you?"

His name stings me. "Hudson? Why would you bring Hudson into this?"

"He told you I was a blubbering mess at my appointment, didn't he? That I was all over the place? My god, I don't know what came over me. I swear, Wills, I cry, like, twenty-four hours a freaking day. I've had people stop me in the street to ask if I'm dying. Literally. *If. I'm. Dying.* That's how hard I'm crying on random Thursdays at two p.m. while I shop for avocados at the grocery store. Because one of the avocados was lonely, and what if my baby is lonely because they're all alone in there?"

She's tearing up just saying it, and I'm a terrible friend because I didn't know any of this until just now. Just now, as I'm about to interrogate her about potentially having an affair with my husband.

"I even started making up a pet cat that died just so I don't seem so pathetic. And then I started crying because I actually wanted a pet cat!" She waves a hand in the air dramatically.

"No, Murphy, stop. Hudson didn't tell me anything about your appointment. He wouldn't. This isn't about that."

"It's okay, I'm not going to, like, *report* him or anything, obviously. I can totally see why he'd be worried. And why you would. But I'm fine, I swear. I just... You know. I'm conflicted about my decision. Conflicted about everything, really. Trust me, though, talking to the baby's father wouldn't help. I don't want him in my child's life."

"Why, though? How can you be certain?"

"I just am," she snips, leaning back. "Why does it matter? Why are you being so pushy about this?"

"Why won't you just give me a name?"

"Because I don't want to. Give me one reason why you need to know."

*"Because it's Hudson, isn't it?"* I squeeze my eyes shut, shouting the question.

When silence follows, I open my eyes again. As they land on her, I find her staring at me with horror and disbelief. Then a hand goes to her mouth and she releases something like a mixture between a sob and a laugh.

*"Hudson?* Are you mad? You honestly think Hudson is the father of my child?" The shock fades away, quickly replaced with indignation. "Is this a joke? How *dare* you? How dare you say that to me? What exactly are you accusing me of? You think I slept with your husband?

You really think I'm capable of that?" Every sentence seems to lose a bit more of the power she had in the beginning.

"I don't know what to think. You won't talk to me." I can't bear to look at her as I say the words. When I finally do, her eyes are filled with glassy tears. They fall quickly, painting lines down her round cheeks.

"How can you possibly think I would do that to you? Or to Hudson, for that matter? He's like my brother. You're my sister. My best friend." She stands from the couch, her words now choked by sobs. "I mean, I know you think I'm some kind of screwup, but honestly, this? You must really think I'm a terrible person and shit friend, hmm?"

"No, of course not." I stand up, too.

"No? *Really?* Because when I'm missing something, I assume I lost it somewhere, not that you stole it. When Trevor broke up with me, I assumed it was because he wanted to go on tour with his band and I was weighing him down, not that he'd fallen in love with you. We're supposed to be best friends, Wills—"

"*We are!*"

"No. Apparently not. You're the *only* person I've had in my life consistently since I was ten years old. Why the hell would I ruin that by sleeping with Hudson? And Jesus Christ. Why can't you see what's right in front of your face? Hudson's *obsessed* with you. You guys are, like, the perfect couple. It's disgusting, frankly. You've never left the honeymoon phase, and if I didn't love you so much, I'd hate you for it. Why would either of us want to hurt you? And he's not even my type! God, I can't believe you're asking me this. I can't believe you thought it."

"Please don't cry. I didn't mean to upset you. I just had to ask."

"Didn't mean to upset me," she says under her breath. She swipes away fresh tears, then blinks as if realizing something. Her eyes widen, and she looks up at me. "Why would you need to ask, Willa? Why would you ever think that? Where is any of this coming from?"

"I..." I'm not sure how to tell her the truth. Not sure if I want to. I make my way toward the door and reach for my purse, digging around until I locate the tape recorder. Turning back to her, I hold it out. "This was delivered to my office yesterday."

"Okay..." She stares at it with a deep wrinkle drawn across her forehead. "What is it?"

"It's a tape recorder."

"Obviously. What's on it?"

I press play and watch her face carefully as her voice comes across the tape. Outright horror envelops her eyes as she stares at it, then at me. Her lips press into a thin line, body rigid and closed off.

When the tape ends, she waits. "Was that all?"

"That's where it ends, yes. Do you know what this is from?"

She rests both hands on her lower back, her mouth slumped open. "I can't believe you have that. I can't believe that asshole recorded me."

"Who recorded you? Who were you talking to on this tape?" I ask, keeping the request as gentle as I can.

Her hands drop back to her sides. "It's... I was talking to my therapist."

"You have a therapist?" This is news to me.

"Don't make this a big deal, okay? I've been going to therapy since I found out I was pregnant to try to process everything. All my issues with my parents, my fears about the pregnancy, all the damn crying."

"Why would I make that a big deal? That's incredible, Murphy. Why wouldn't you tell me?"

"I wasn't ready to talk about it, I guess. It was my thing, you know? Talking about it made it feel permanent. Like a fixture in my life. *Therapy.*" She shudders at the word. "God, here I thought I was being responsible, and then he goes and does this. If he has that tape, what else has he recorded? Everything?" She presses a fist to her lips, thinking. "And why would he send it to you?"

"I have no idea. Obviously, someone thought I needed to hear it. Why would they think that if you weren't talking about Hudson?"

"Oh my god." She groans, stomping her foot. "I have no idea, but I wasn't. I'm not sleeping with your husband, okay? Can you just, for one second, give me time to process the fact that my private, intimate conversations are being recorded and given to people without my permission? Can we just move on from your problems for once?"

I jolt back as if I've been slapped. Perhaps I deserve what she's saying, but that doesn't make it sting any less. "I'm sorry. I don't mean to make this all about myself. I understand how violated you must feel."

"*How violated...*" She huffs, shaking her head. "Yeah, I guess you could call it that. You just don't get it. You'll never get it. I was trying to get better for once in my life. I decided it was finally time to work through my issues. Most importantly, to decide whether or not I'm ready to be a mom. To know that he used that against me, that he betrayed me..." She turns away from me, makes her way back to her water bottle on the counter, and takes a drink. I suspect she doesn't want me to see that she's crying again, so I stay back.

"You need to take this tape to the police, Murphy. You could sue him. What he's done isn't right. It could get you out of this place, set you up somewhere better. You wouldn't have to struggle so much."

"I don't want to do that. You're still not getting it. I don't want to be the victim. If I go forward with this, it would mean admitting I needed help in the first place. I couldn't even tell my best friend. Do you really think I'm ready to tell the world?"

"I'm so sorry you didn't feel like you could tell me about therapy. I would've been so happy for you. I *am* happy for you. There is nothing to be ashamed of."

She grasps the counter, her back to me. "I know that. I know that's what people say. What you would say. I've thought about telling you so many times."

"Then why didn't you? Have I done something to make you feel—"

"No. God, no. *Willa!*" She spins around, suddenly angry. Exasperated. "It's not about you. It has nothing to do with you, okay? I didn't tell you because I hate *always* feeling like the one who's falling apart—"

"What are you talking about?"

"Don't do that." She shoves her hands down to her sides, cheeks red. "Don't patronize me."

"I'm not—"

"Just stop, okay? We're the same age. Went to the same school, lived in the same town. But you graduated from college and I didn't. And then you got married and I didn't. You got your life together. Moved on from everything. And I didn't."

"That's not true."

"*It is.* As much as I love you, as much as I appreciate you, the weight of feeling like the hot-mess friend all the time is a lot. And I don't tell you these things because I know if I do, you're just going to try to make me feel better, which would only really make me feel worse. I just wanted to get things figured out on my own. I've been trying to get a promotion at the bar. Assistant manager or something. It's not much, but it would mean more money. No more living on tips. I'd have a real salary. It would mean I could leave this dump and get a real place. Something that feels like mine. I've been saving and eating less takeout. I've really been trying, and then *this* happened." She gestures to her stomach. "One stupid slipup, and suddenly all my progress was out the window. And no matter what I've done, I'm back to being the hot mess. The screwup. The one you have to come and rescue. Again. Like you always have."

She hangs her head down, and I resist the urge to

comfort her. No matter what I say, it feels like it will be the wrong thing. "I just wanted to save myself for once."

"Murphy, I've never seen you as a screwup." I'm not sure if it's a lie, but she seems to think it is.

"Except at the first hint that I was sleeping with a married man, you automatically assumed it must be your husband. You've known me all your life, and it still wasn't enough for you to stop and think maybe, just maybe, I'm not *that* terrible of a person."

"What else was I supposed to think? Why else would someone have sent me that tape? Whatever you assume, however judgmental you think I am, that is not how I see you. I just don't know what else to think." Tears sting my own eyes now, and I realize what I've done. I was so blinded by my own terror, my own insecurities that I didn't stop to question any of it. "I love you. I'm so sorry. I'm so, so sorry. For all of it. For ever making you feel like a hot mess, for questioning you. For—"

"You should go, Wills." She bites her bottom lip, crossing her arms over her chest and looking away as a fat tear rolls down her cheek. "I need to clean up my apartment."

"I can help."

"No. Thank you, but no. I'd like to be alone."

A whimper escapes my throat. "I'm so sorry. I don't know what I was thinking. I was just so scared—"

"Lots of us are scared. Every day. But, if you think I'm the kind of friend who would stab you in the back like that... I don't know. Maybe I just need to figure out what the hell I'm doing with my life."

"I don't think that," I assure her. "Murphy, I'm sorry. Look at me. I was scared. I got this"—I hold out the recorder—"and I didn't know what else it could mean. It was a gut reaction."

"Except you said you got it yesterday, so you've had a whole night to think about it and this was still the conclusion you jumped to. I just... I need a minute, okay? Please just leave."

"I don't want to leave you alone."

She shrugs with new tears in her eyes. I hate it as much as I hate myself. "Turns out, I've always been alone." She moves to the door and holds it open as I pick up my purse and make my way out slowly. I want to fight, to argue, to tell her we have to work it out like we always do, but she has no fight left in her. I can see it in her eyes as she meets mine one last time.

Then she shuts the door.

# CHAPTER TWENTY-FIVE

## HUDSON

The prison sentence for threatening someone with a gun depends on the charge. As a misdemeanor, the jail time can range from three months to a year in county jail. As a felony, it's up to three years in state prison. Charges for prostitution could add another fifteen years to my sentence.

It would be hard to prove, but not impossible. June is powerful enough I wouldn't put anything past her, including fabricating evidence if what she has isn't enough, though she already has a lot.

Besides the incriminating photos, she has Maddie's contact info and the website Maddie runs with our profiles on them. It's discreet enough, but if you know what you're looking for, it's obvious what the site is.

There are payments going into my account I could never explain.

If June just makes the accusation, there would probably be enough to pin me even without the photos. I'm assuming that would be her plan so as not to implicate herself.

If, instead, she were to tell the police she was with a lover and I came in and attacked them, what excuse would I have for being there? They could say I'd followed them into the room. Tried to rob them. That's what prostitutes do, after all, isn't it?

Even if she had to admit she'd solicited me, though I imagine she'd find a way around that, she'd have an expensive lawyer to get her off and the jury's sympathy. She'd probably work out a deal before it ever went to trial.

I can practically hear her now, telling them how lonely she's been since her husband's death, how she just wanted solace for the night.

There are a lot of moving pieces and things that wouldn't totally add up, but with the resources and connections she has, there is no doubt in my mind I will go down for this if she wants me to.

Maybe she'll just kill me instead.

If I turn myself in, the worst-case scenario is that I'm looking at eighteen years. Maybe less if I cut a deal. I would be twenty years older. I'd lose my medical license. My house. Possibly my wife.

I could deal with everything except losing Willa, I think. Though, if she was happy, safe, maybe it would all have been worth it.

I should've walked away from this years ago. Should've never made the suggestion that I pick it back up when we needed extra money for a car repair or a plumbing emergency.

This is my fault in the only way it can be anyone's fault. June is wealthy. Influential. She's untouchable, as far as I can tell. And she will stop at nothing to take what she wants from us.

Unless I put an end to it.

Unless I tell her there is nothing left for her to take.

Extortion is a worse crime than either of mine, but she will no doubt have lawyer upon lawyer ready to defend her story of being a perfect citizen.

It's a classic case of powerful people against the rest of us, and I'm no exception to the rule. She will win, and we will pay.

I can't chance it.

Can't risk Willa's life or her freedom. I won't let June hurt her.

When I hear the front door close, I exit the browser and leave the office. My wife looks exhausted, standing in the living room with a weary expression and disheveled hair and clothes. When she sees me, the stress melts away like butter. Passed to me.

I will gladly take it.

I outstretch my arms and pull her into me, kissing the top of her head. Without warning, she breaks down into sobs.

"What is it?" I whisper. "What happened?" What sort of trip to the grocery store could end with her in such a state?

"I went to visit Murphy."

Oh.

"And?"

"She said awful things, Hudson."

"She didn't mean them."

"She did." She pulls away, wiping her eyes. "And she was right."

"Right about what?" I lower myself to her level, trying to understand.

"She said that I patronize her. That I try to save her. That I make her feel like she can't do anything on her own."

"Sweetheart, it's just because you care about her. She knows that—"

"I asked her about the affair."

I nod and shove my hands in my pockets. "I assumed you would."

"She denied it."

"Because it's not true."

"But I still believed it was. Even after you told me it wasn't—"

"Because that's what men always say." I offer her a sympathetic grin. "Willa, as much as I hoped you would believe me, I do understand that while we have a bit of an unconventional marriage, we aren't above slipping into the same patterns other marriages do. If you had to check with Murphy, it doesn't bother me. I am not the father of her child. We are not having an affair. But I don't blame you for wanting to double-check my story. If the situation were reversed, I'd probably want to do the same."

"I did. And she didn't take it well."

"How is she?"

"She made me leave."

"She'll calm down."

"She won't."

I sit down on the couch and pull her onto my lap. "She will. She'll calm down and you'll apologize, and it will all be okay. Tensions are just high right now." I kiss her head, then her lips. "I need you to promise me you'll make up with her, okay?" I suck in a breath to hide my voice cracking. "She needs you as much as you need her."

She dries her eyes. "I will."

"Good." I let her rest against my chest for a long while, her head rising and falling against my cheek. I could stay like this for the rest of my life and never want anything more. "Listen, I was thinking about what we talked about. About how we should get away for a while."

"We agreed that wouldn't work." She pulls back, eyeing me.

"Yeah. Well, I think it's worth a try. We could go to Hawaii like we've always talked about. Or Greece. Wherever you want."

"But what about June?"

"We could leave in the middle of the night. Drive to Florida or North Carolina. Maine. California. Name a place, and we'll go." My voice breaks, but this time I can't hide it.

She studies me for a long while, and I do everything in my power to keep my face steady. Strong.

"Where is this coming from?"

"We've just both been under so much pressure lately. I thought maybe a week away could be good for us."

"No." She slips off my lap in a hurry, then sits down on the ottoman, her fists clenched at her sides.

"What?"

"No. I know what you're doing."

"What are you talking about?"

"You're going to turn yourself in, aren't you? You're planning to give up! To leave me!"

I put my hands up, reaching for her in an attempt to calm her down. "Breathe. I'm not leaving you. I would never, could never, leave you. I'm doing this *for* you."

"Well, don't. I didn't ask you to. I don't want you to. This isn't what I want. She doesn't get to win."

"She's not winning. If I turn myself in, she doesn't get the baby. She may even get in trouble herself for blackmailing us. She wins nothing, and we are safe."

"Safe? How does this make either of us safe? You'd be in jail, and if she tells the police about the fire, I will go to jail, too."

"I could get community service. Or cut a deal for just a year or two, especially if I'm cooperative. I've never hurt anyone. Maybe they'll even believe my story and I'll get no jail time at all. And as for you, the fire happened a long time ago. She could never prove it was your fault."

"How do you know that? The worst thing we can do right now is underestimate her. Hasn't she proven that enough?"

"I know." I rub my lips together, trying to think. To figure out the best way to sell her on this. I need her to agree, and we don't have much time. "That's exactly why it could work. It's the one thing she's not counting on. She doesn't believe I'll turn myself in, and that's why I think this is our best option."

"It's not an option. No. I can't lose you," she cries, tears painting her cheeks again.

Knife, meet heart.

I gather her in my arms, wishing so badly I could make this all better. "You never will. Do you hear me? You could never lose me."

"We will get her a baby, Hudson. Please just give me another week. Please. I will talk to Murphy. I'll make this work."

It's not the right solution, but it's what she wants. What she needs. It feels wrong to agree, but making her happy? Even if it's for the last time, nothing has ever felt more right.

# CHAPTER TWENTY-SIX

## WILLA

Later that afternoon, while Hudson showers upstairs, I'm replaying the fight with Murphy again. I was so sure she might know June. That maybe June had been following her. That they might've even interacted at one point.

But that theory, like everything else, was a dead end.

I need to find out how June knows about the fire. It feels like that's the key to everything, though I still can't figure it out.

On my phone, I pull up the article Hudson showed me the other night. There's not much coverage on it, not like if it would've happened now. A single local newspaper picked up the story.

I can't bring myself to read through the entire thing. I've never been able to. It's too much.

I close out of the article, struck by a new idea. I've looked into June so much, but since she mentioned the fire to Hudson, I've been so filled with panic, I haven't thought to research a possible connection between her and that night.

*There has to be a connection, doesn't there?* No amount of following me would've pointed her toward the fire. *Why didn't I see it before?*

Opening the search engine, I type: **June Cromwell Nashville house fire**

The first results are about June now. Her businesses. Her husband's obituary. The result I need is near the bottom. So insignificant I almost miss it.

But I don't.

And suddenly, everything makes sense.

---

*"We need to meet,"* I practically shout at her when she answers the phone. My voice echoes in the quiet kitchen.

"I'm afraid that won't be possible, as I have made perfectly clear."

I squeeze my phone, imagining for a brief second that it's her neck. "Yeah, well, I need you to make it possible."

She laughs. "What do you want, Willa? I'm busy."

"I want to talk about why you sent this tape to me, *June*," I spit her name back at her.

"Tape? I have no idea what you're talking about."

"Oh, I think you do."

"There are quite a lot of tapes in this world. Scotch tape. Packaging tape. Duct tape. Medical tape. I'm afraid you'll have to be more specific."

"The tape *recorder* from one of Murphy's therapy sessions."

"Who is Murphy? It's not ringing any bells."

"Why did you send it to me? Did you want me to believe she was sleeping with my husband? Is that your game plan? Break me and Hudson up? Cause us to stop trusting each other? Because it won't work. Do you hear me? It won't work." I jab my finger into the wood of the table.

"Again"—she pauses with a huff—"I have no idea what you could mean."

"I know it was you who sent it—"

"*But* if there is such a tape—and I was the one who sent it—I, for one, can't understand why you would be bothered by it at all. Would a rendezvous with your best friend really be any different than the cheating he does every other night?"

So, she does know who Murphy is after all. My chest tightens, and I lean forward over the table, lowering my mouth as close as possible to the speaker. "My husband is not a cheater."

"Getting paid for it doesn't make it any less sex. I presume it's the sex you're angry about, not the cuddling afterward. The sweet nothings whispered into her ear."

"They didn't have sex, and this is none of your business. Stay away from my friends. And my family."

"Seems like I have a right to look out for *my* family, don't you think?"

Her words steal my breath.

"*Your* family?"

"It is Murphy's baby I'll be receiving, isn't it? Through my one-hundred-percent *legal* adoption."

"How could you know that?"

"Oh, please. You have one friend, Willa. And none of the clients at your agency have matched what you've told me. It's only right I keep tabs on the woman who's giving birth to my child."

"No." I lick my chapped lips, my leg jiggling underneath me. "No, you're wrong. It's not her."

"Am I? Then, who is it? I'm going to need a name."

"She's a client."

"A name, then?" she repeats. "Please."

"I can't reveal that to you."

"Suit yourself. But I'm going to have to continue keeping eyes on Murphy as sort of an insurance policy, don't you think?"

"No, I don't *think*. She has nothing to do with any of this." I lean my head into my hand.

"Well, I'm sorry to say I just don't trust you anymore. It's not like you're a beacon of honesty."

"And you are?"

"*I've never killed anyone*," she snaps, her voice feral and so unlike anything I've ever heard from her.

My spine straightens almost without warning. "That's what this is about, isn't it?"

"Nine people died in the fire that you started. Kids. Nine kids."

Her words do as she intends, stabbing me squarely in the chest, the pain from that night back as real and sharp as ever.

I swallow. "Including your son."

Her silence is a confirmation.

"It was an accident, June," I whisper. "I never meant for anyone to get hurt. I never meant for your son to get hurt. You have to know that."

"Don't you dare speak of him. Whether or not you intended for people to get hurt, they did. My son did. You started a fire at that party, and then you left it. You left the house and didn't look back."

"That's not true! I tried to get them to leave! I tried!" I sob, the night replaying in my mind again, as it has so many nights in the past.

"Not hard enough."

I can't catch my breath. My hand goes to my throat, my lungs fighting for air. "I was just a kid. I was scared!"

"Don't you think they were scared?"

I pound a hand onto the kitchen table, bitter tears blurring my vision. "So, what? Why are you doing this? What do you want from me?"

"Exactly what you stole."

I suck in a breath. "This baby will not replace your son."

"Don't speak about things you don't understand. I don't know how you know, but yes, my son died in that fire, Willa. The fire you started. The fire you left. The fire you survived. He was upstairs playing video games with his friends, and by the time they realized the house was on fire, there was no escape route left. He burned up in that house, afraid and alone. You took him from me. So now, you will give me exactly what you stole. And nothing less."

"I..." Tears fill my eyes. I don't want it to be true. I wanted her to tell me what I read online was wrong. And yet, somewhere deep down inside of me, I knew it wasn't. I know the kind of pain in her voice can only come from someplace real. A place I know all too well. "June, I'm so sorry."

"Save it."

"I tried so hard. I swear to you, I did. It all happened so fast. I tried—"

"I'm not interested in your empty apologies. I've spent years waiting for my chance to get my revenge on the person responsible. My son, my Nathan, will never come back to me, but you *will* get me a new child, or I will turn this recording in to the police."

My heart stops. I can no longer breathe. No longer think. I'm not entirely sure I'm still awake. "What did you say?"

"You heard me. I recorded this little conversation. Hope you don't mind. And I'd be more than happy to turn the portion where you admit to your crime over to the police, should it come to that. You see, unlike you, Willa, when I try to do something, I get it done."

With that, the line goes dead.

# CHAPTER TWENTY-SEVEN

## HUDSON

"I need to tell you something."

The sound of Willa's voice behind me causes me to jump. I catch her reflection in the foggy bathroom mirror and spin around, finding her waiting in the doorway.

She looks as though she's been crying again.

"I thought you were taking a nap."

"I lied," she says. Simple. Matter of fact. Apparently the lie isn't the worst of it.

"Why did you—"

"I went downstairs to do more research. And then I called June."

"You did *what*? Why?"

"Because I knew there had to be a connection. Her knowing about the fire doesn't make sense. It was so long ago and I've done everything to separate myself from it. For her to know, there had to be a connection. I knew there was. And I was right. I found it."

I'm not sure I understand. "You found what?"

She inhales a shaky, uneven breath. "She... Um... Her son... Hudson, her son died the night of the fire."

Time seems to move in slow motion as I process what she's saying. "Her *son?*"

"He was one of the kids in the house. I... I know I said I wasn't ready before. To talk about it after you found out, I mean. But I am now. I have to be."

"Okay. Yeah. Let's just... Here, let me grab some clothes and then we can talk." She follows me to the bedroom, where I drop my towel in the hamper and quickly pull on the first things I can find. She's waiting for me on the bed when I sit down. "Whenever you're ready."

She stares around the room with a glassy-eyed look, not saying anything for a long time. I suspect she's rehearsing what she's about to tell me. When she finally opens her mouth, her voice is low. It's as if she regrets every word before it's said.

"We weren't, um, supposed to be there that night. I told my parents I was staying at Murphy's. Her mom was working late, so she wouldn't have known the difference, but we left her a note that we were staying at another girl's house—Serena's—just in case she came home early and noticed we weren't there. It was just supposed to be a house party. We'd been to them a hundred times since I'd turned sixteen and gotten a car. We got there late. Around nine or ten, I think. The party was already going and there were more kids there than usual."

She licks her lips, running a hand across them slowly. "It was rowdy, you know? So much so that it scared me a little bit. Murphy and I ended up hiding out with Serena and a few random guys from school in an upstairs bedroom. We were just drinking at first. I don't even remember what. Someone cut a can of beer open once it had been emptied, and we filled it with random liquor, passing it around and drinking out of that."

I wince, trying hard not to let the image fill my mind. It's strange picturing my wife that way. Young and carefree. Less than perfect.

"One of the guys brought pot, so at some point, we all started smoking his joint. It made me sick, though. I'd never smoked before, but I didn't want to seem like, I don't know, a prude or whatever, so I went along with it. I'll never understand how people like the stuff. Maybe it just doesn't work for me, because the only thing it did was make me miserably sick. It was like the whole room started spinning and I barely made it to the bathroom in time. I must've been in there for an hour. Like, picture *Exorcist*-level vomiting."

I reach out a hand, rubbing my fingers over hers slowly. Silently, I'm telling her I'm still here.

"When I came back to the bedroom, Serena and all of the guys but one were gone. They'd spilled alcohol all over the carpet. It smelled like nail polish remover in there." She winces. "I can still smell it."

Her nose wrinkles at the memory.

"Murphy was trying to light up another joint, or maybe it was a cigarette. I don't even remember now, but she was wasted and clumsy. We all were, plus I was still nauseous. It all happened so fast. I looked up, and she was starting to fall over. She moved her hand to catch herself." She mimics the movement in slow motion, lost in the memory. "The flame from the lighter touched the carpet, and it just went up. In seconds, I swear. It spread across the carpet and up the curtains. The bed. We tried to put it out. The guy... I don't even remember his name now. He bailed when he realized it wasn't working, but I kept trying. I took off my jacket and tried to smother it like I'd seen people do in movies and stuff."

She pauses, rubbing her lips together. "Maybe if I hadn't been so drunk, so sick, I could've done more. When I realized it was out of control, that I couldn't stop it, I grabbed Murphy. She was so out of it at that point I practically had to drag her down the stairs. I shouted for someone to help, but no one came."

Her words are spilling out faster now, picking up speed as if they were the flames gathering momentum themselves. "I couldn't find Serena or any of the guys we'd been upstairs with. I was shouting that there was a fire, that we needed to get out, to call the police, but it was so loud... The music... The people... No one was listening. *No one would listen to me.* I was dizzy and sick and weak, and I just... I needed to save her, you know? I needed to get us out. I told myself if I could just get her out of the house, I could come back and do more. I tried to tell every person on my way to the door that there was a fire, that they needed to leave. A few people eventually heard me, but... It wasn't enough. I should've called the police, the fire department, but once I got outside, once I caught my breath, the entire upstairs was filled with smoke and it looked like everyone was leaving."

She blinks back tears, a hand moving to clutch her throat. "I think that was when it set in for me. The reality of what had happened. I was so scared I would be blamed. That my parents would find out I'd lied to them. That I'd been at the party. They already didn't like Murphy or her mom. I knew if they found out what happened, I'd never be able to see her again."

She sighs, dropping her shoulders. "So, I walked us to my car a few blocks away and we fell asleep. I couldn't drive. I wouldn't do that. When we woke up the next morning, the house had burned down almost completely. After I got home that afternoon, I remember hearing on the news that some of the kids hadn't made it out."

The ghosts of the memories are clearly evident in her eyes. *How have I missed them for so long?*

"I never told anyone what happened. I was too horri-fied by what I'd done. If I'd called the fire department that night, maybe they would've been able to save everyone."

"Maybe," I agree. The sound of my voice seems to spook her. "But you don't know that. You can't blame yourself for what happened. You didn't start the fire. You saved Murphy, warned people. You did all you could."

"Except call for help. I saved myself instead. How could I have been so selfish?"

It's obvious now how much this has eaten her alive.

"Willa, you didn't know. You tried. You were just a kid. You were drunk. You weren't thinking straight. Yes, it's a tragic accident. Yes, it's terrible that those kids died, but you didn't cause the fire. You don't deserve to have this weight on your conscience."

"But don't you get it? *This* is why June is doing what she is."

"What are you talking about?"

She tucks a piece of hair behind her ear, gathering her hands in her lap. "She says I owe her a son for the one I took from her. I'm the reason all of this is happening, not you." With a sharp, regret-filled breath, she adds, "I never looked into the families. I should've. If I'd known her son was in that fire, I would've realized that's what all this was about. I was just so scared to look into it back then. I couldn't even attend their funerals. I was terrified the police would become suspicious of me, and I never wanted to give them a reason to."

"It's not your fault," I say.

"Yes. Yes, it is. It's not *your* fault, Hudson. Don't you see that? You were collateral damage on her path to get to me. To make me pay for what I did. Whether or not it's my fault, it's definitely not yours. I can't let you go down for this."

"You weren't the one who went to the hotel that night. In fact, you didn't want me to go, if I remember correctly."

"Yes, but *I'm* the guilty one. Not you. You did nothing wrong."

"What I did—what I *do*—is illegal. We've always known that and chosen to live with the risks. Do I think it's shit that it's illegal? Absolutely. If it were legal, it could be done much safer, with proper protocols. But it's not. That was my choice. Neither of us is completely innocent here, maybe, but neither of us deserves what June is doing either. I'm sorry, Willa, I'm not going to let you martyr yourself. We're in this together. That's what you said."

"But you've been honest about everything from the start. I always knew what you do. I knew where you were going and what you were doing that night. You've always been up front with me. I *lied* to you. I've been lying to you about this for years. Keeping it from you. How can you ever look at me the same?"

I don't have a choice.

I see it now.

She needs to know the whole truth.

Everything.

I take a breath, preparing myself for what's to come. I swore to Murphy I'd never tell, but now I need to. For all of our sakes. "No, Willa, you're wrong."

"About what?"

"I lied to you, too."

Her eyes widen, distracting her from her pain momentarily. "No, you didn't."

"I did. When I... When I told you I'd never slept with Murphy, I lied."

Her hands ball into fists. "No."

"Yes. I'm so sorry. We never meant to—"

"So, it's true? Really? I told you if I ever found out... I gave you the chance to tell me the truth, and you said—"

"I know, but it's not what you think. We aren't having

an affair." I reach for her hands, smoothing out her fists. "I slept with her before we'd ever met. Before I knew you existed."

"What are you talking about? That doesn't make any sense."

"She came into the bar one night when I was working, looking for a job. We didn't have any openings, but we hit it off. It was just one night. But..." I suck in another breath. *Here goes nothing.* "She got pregnant."

Tears brim her eyes as she stares at me, unblinking. "Wha..."

"She had an abortion as soon as she found out. I went with her. Held her hand. It was... We were never in love. Never had feelings for each other, even. We never spoke again after that night. Which is why, once you and I became so close, when I met her again a few months in and you introduced her as your best friend, I knew if I ever wanted a chance with you, I had to be careful about how I told you. I know we weren't dating then, but I was madly in love with you. You knew that. In the end, Murphy and I decided it was too heavy a thing to tell you. We both knew how much it would hurt you, confuse you. We didn't want it to complicate things when it meant so little to us."

She nods, still unblinking. Frankly, I'm not even sure she's heard what I'm saying.

"We agreed not to tell you to protect you, but I do know how wrong that was. Every single day, I've thought about it. It kills me. The lie. I wish I could go back and tell you right away. Just come clean about it from the start. But every day that passed just made it harder to do. And when I knew you were the one, once I proposed, I had to accept that I could never tell you. I understand if you hate me or if I've lost your trust, but please believe me when I tell you it was *one* time. One single time. It meant nothing to me. Or to her, for that matter. We've never spoken of it since except to say we didn't want to hurt you." I drop my head forward into my hands. "Which I can see now we've done anyway. Please... Please say something."

She opens her mouth, but no sound comes out. Finally, she stands, a hand held out to indicate that I shouldn't follow her as she leaves the room.

I stand, too, but I respect her wishes not to follow. Not yet.

Perhaps I've just made the biggest mistake of my life, but at least this way, the truth is out there.

The lie has been eating away at me, but I would've sat through the peril every day to avoid passing the pain to her.

Was any of it worth it?

How did we end up here?

What the hell are we going to do next?

# CHAPTER TWENTY-EIGHT

## WILLA

I don't speak to Hudson for the rest of the evening. I can't. When he finally leaves our bedroom, I return to find solace under the covers. It's not that I'm angry, really. It's that I don't even know what to say.

I'm hurt.

I'm humiliated.

How many times did my husband and my best friend sit in the same room as me, with this giant secret between them, while I lived obliviously in the dark?

Then again, when I told Hudson my whole truth, everything that happened that night, he responded with nothing but grace and kindness.

He forgave me before I ever had to ask for forgiveness. He gave me excuses I didn't deserve and grace I've never earned.

The longer I lie in bed, the angrier I get with myself. The angrier with myself I feel, the more the emptiness takes over.

That's what I feel. Empty. Empty of my secret, which has weighed me down for more than eleven years now. Empty of hope. Empty of faith that this will all work out. Empty of a reason to want it to.

Once, I'd believed we had an enviable marriage. Even with our quirks, I love my husband more than life, and there's nothing in me that doubts he feels the same way. We have more love and happiness in our home than we could ever ask for.

Still, it isn't enough. It isn't enough to shield us from the horror waiting. From the secrets and lies that are determined to ruin us.

Will I let them? I don't know.

What will any of it matter if June turns us in to the police anyway? Will all of this heartache have been for nothing?

Maybe this is what I deserve after what I did. For eleven years, I've gotten away with it. I've built a life, a marriage, a home. More than those nine kids ever did.

I roll over in bed, staring at the wall.

I just want it all to stop.

I just wish I could make it stop.

---

When I wake up next, I have no idea what day or time it is. It's still dark outside, but on the floor next to the bed is a tray of food and a glass of water.

I groan, throwing the covers back and leaning over.

When I do, a wave of nausea hits me. It's been too long since I last ate.

All of the foods on the tray are breakfast items. Toast. Eggs. Bacon. It must be very early morning. I must've slept all night. Did I eat anything yesterday? I can't remember, if so.

I check my phone. No calls or texts from Murphy, though I'm not surprised. I take a sip of the water, which has a bitter, stale taste in my dry mouth, and a bite of toast. My stomach growls at the welcome meal.

Then, all at once, my stomach clenches, my body ice cold. My jaw chatters with a rush of adrenaline.

*I'm going to be sick.*

I shove myself up off the bed and rush to the bathroom, narrowly making it in time to lift the lid on the toilet and crane my neck over it.

Alone, I puke up the minuscule contents of my stomach, crying for myself and my marriage, my past, and my best friend.

When I'm done, I press my face to the cool tile of the floor, listening to the sound of my own heartbeat.

*Thump-thump.*

*Thump-thump.*

*Thump-thump.*

It carries on, despite all reasons to stop.

I hear the door open, see his feet come into view. His faded blue socks, the pajama pants with tattered hems from dragging on the ground.

I squeeze my eyes shut, like I can make myself disappear if I'm just still enough.

"Are you alright?" He crouches down next to me, placing a hand on my side. Opening the door under the sink, he pulls out a washcloth, stands to soak it in warm water, then uses it to dab my mouth.

When he pulls his hand away, my eyes land on the open door under the sink.

More specifically, the box of tampons sitting just inside the door. I swallow down the bitter taste of vomit in my throat.

*No.*

*No.*

*No.*

# CHAPTER TWENTY-NINE

## HUDSON

On my way home from the grocery store Sunday morning, I contemplate what I've done. Telling her my secret may have been a terrible mistake, but it felt right in the moment.

The truth is, I've carried the weight of what happened between Murphy and me since the day I realized she was close to Willa. Everything I told my wife is true. I never meant to hurt her. If there had been a way to bring it up the day she introduced Murphy as her best friend, I would've.

I've looked back over that day so many times, filled with regret, wondering how I somehow could've told her the truth in a way that wouldn't have ended in disaster. But, if I had, would I have lost her? Pushed her away before I ever even had her? Would it have been too much then?

How should I have brought it up? In between

learning her middle name and telling her why I prefer vanilla ice cream over chocolate? We were still so new, even in our friendship. It felt like if I broke the news, no matter how I did, it was sure to be too much, too soon.

It would've been all too easy for her to walk away.

If I knew this was the only way to get her to stay with me, the only choice that would bring us to this moment, I wouldn't have changed a thing. Our marriage, however fleeting it may turn out to be, has changed my life.

I consider texting Murphy to give her a heads-up that I've broken our pact, but I don't. I don't want to involve myself or step on Willa's decision-making. If she wants to discuss it with Murphy, she will in her own time.

Back at the house, I walk through the front door with the grocery bags in my arms and place them on the kitchen floor.

I've bought some of her favorite things: rocky road ice cream, Sour Patch Kids, and a bottle of cabernet. I put them away, along with the salmon I picked up for dinner and the other odds and ends for the house, before making my way to the bedroom.

When I open the door, I find her sitting up in our bed.

Progress.

At least she's in an upright position.

Without speaking, I cross the room and sit down on the end of the bed. When she looks up at me, I notice her lips are still chapped. The glass of water I brought her hasn't been touched. She's not getting enough to drink.

To my surprise, the anger that has been in her eyes since I told her the truth is gone. She draws her knees into her chest, wrapping her arms around herself.

"We need to talk."

Her voice sounds almost unrecognizable to me, hoarse from throwing up and nearly a full day of not being used.

"Can I go first?" I put a hand on my chest. "I'm so sorry for lying to you, Willa. It's been the hardest thing in the world for me, but I just didn't know how to tell you. I love you and I care about Murphy because of who she is to you, but I knew from the moment I met you that you were special. And telling you about us when we were so new, telling you something so terrible... I was scared I would lose you. I couldn't risk that. I understand if you can never forgive me, but—"

"I'm late."

The room falls silent at her outburst. It feels like I'm driving on ice, as if the car has lost control and we've veered dangerously off course.

"You're what?"

"I'm late," she repeats before licking her lips. "I just realized this morning when I got sick."

The car has flipped now, and I'm upside down. My head pounds. My heart hammers against my rib cage like it wants out. "You're... Are you..."

She meets my eyes again. "I'm not."

Relief. The car stops. The world stops. This is not the tragedy I thought it was.

"I'm not pregnant, but I thought I was."

"How could you know?"

"I had an extra test under the sink from when Murphy took her test here. She bought a three pack, but she only used two." She dips her head, chin tucked against her chest.

"Okay." I can't understand the look on her face when she looks back up at me. "Are you okay? Did you... Did you hope it would be positive?"

"No." Her answer comes quickly. "No, I didn't, but for just a little while, I contemplated the possibility that it would be. I tried to figure out what that would mean for us. For our future."

Our future. She's still talking about our future.

"The thing is, for a brief millisecond, I thought maybe our problem was solved. I thought we could give June our baby, and we could leave Murphy out of this." A dry, humorless laugh escapes her throat. "I thought it was the answer to everything. But, just as quickly, I realized I couldn't do it. I would not give that woman our baby, even if it meant saving us, and so"—she pauses, picking at a stray thread on the comforter—"I cannot give her Murphy's baby, either. Or anyone else's, for that matter." When she looks at me, it's with so much sorrow I feel like I'm deflating. "I'm sorry, Hudson. I don't know what this will mean for either of us, but I can't let an innocent little baby pay for what we've done. I just can't. I think we've both always known it, that's why we've fought so hard to find a way out, but sometimes the only way out is through. I can't give that woman a baby. Any baby. Not when we know what she's capable of. Maybe she was a great mother before, but that isn't who she is now. She's evil. Manipulative."

I reach for her hands, and to my relief, she doesn't pull away. "I know. Hey, listen, I get it. I do."

"I don't know what's going to happen to us."

I pull her into my chest and she falls into place, safe and warm in my arms. The warm scent of her shampoo hits me. Strawberry and mint, a combination I'll never grow tired of. "Let's not think about that right now, okay? Let's just be here."

She nods against my shirt, curling herself into me as close as she can. I hold her so tightly I worry I'm hurting her. "For what it's worth," she whispers, "I forgive you."

Tears sting my eyes. These are the words I've needed to hear for years, but I never realized it until now. "You do?"

"There's nothing to forgive, Hud. I get why you didn't tell me. I hate that you didn't, but I have no room to judge you. I just needed time."

"I know." I rock her back and forth, and suddenly, I'm picturing the baby that almost existed. Picturing us as parents, holding and rocking a little piece of ourselves. Loving them. Watching them grow. "For what it's worth," I repeat her words, "if things were different, I don't think you being pregnant would've been the worst thing."

She sniffles, staying silent for a long while. "I had a similar thought."

"We might get through this," I whisper, choking on my words. "We might be okay." It's a prayer. A wish.

She doesn't respond but nuzzles in closer to me. If today is our last day before it all implodes, I want to spend it right here.

With her.

# CHAPTER THIRTY

## WILLA

We're still in bed, though a few hours have passed now. We've spent all morning together, lying here. Breathing. Existing. Knowing this could be our last chance to live this way.

How do people choose to live their last normal days if given a chance?

For me, it doesn't feel like there's a choice.

I'm too exhausted, too petrified to do much else other than hold on to my husband for dear life and dream of what might've been.

Occasionally, I consider turning on one of our favorite shows, but how much time has been lost to a screen already? How many nights have I scrolled mindlessly through social media rather than picking his mind, learning more about him?

I wish I could take it all back. Every lost moment, every fight, every night I went to sleep without a kiss because we were too exhausted or on separate schedules.

I send silent promises to the universe. If we make it through this, I will never take him for granted again. If we don't go to jail, if I don't lose him, I will soak up and appreciate how beautiful and wonderful our life is.

That's why I have no intention of moving. Though I've chalked my nausea up to stress, the thought of food still turns my stomach. I'm certainly not going to clean my house with what may be my last few hours, and while I intend to say goodbye and apologize to Murphy soon, I can't handle another fight right now.

And she would fight this. I have no doubts about that. If she knew what was happening, I'm scared to consider what she'd do. Would she give up her child willingly? Would she confront June? Either way, she'd tell me we're giving up without a fight, though I don't think that's true. We're fighting in our own way. The only way we know how.

When we tell June we're backing out of this deal, that she can do whatever she wants, but we're done, I'm scared of what she'll do.

Go to the police, maybe. Kill us, possibly. Threaten us, definitely.

So, this is us fighting. Because the alternative is too heavy to bear.

When my phone chimes from across the room, I stay still. I have no interest in seeing what it might be. Eventually, though, habit wins out and I roll over, reaching for my phone on the nightstand.

When I see the name on the screen, my heart rate picks up speed.

"What is it?" Hudson asks.

I sit up, adjusting myself on the bed as I open the text.

It's just a photo. No words. No greeting. No explanation.

"I don't know."

When I look closer, using my fingers to zoom in on the photograph, I realize it's a photo of June and her driver standing outside her car somewhere in public. He's the same man I saw in the parking garage, the one who accompanied her to our house the night she told us there would be no more last-minute visits.

In the photo, he's leaned down close, as if talking to her, whispering maybe, his lips inches from hers. It's uncomfortable to stare at the picture, as if we're interrupting an intimate moment.

Is June sleeping with her driver?

Are we supposed to somehow use this to get her to leave us alone? Threaten him? He's big enough to kill us both—looks mean enough to do it, too—so that's not exactly an appealing option, but I consider it.

How on earth would we even get close enough to him without her around to do that?

"What is that about?" Hudson asks, leaning over my shoulder to get a better look.

"I don't really know. It's from Mike."

His hand comes to rest on my shoulder. "Mike? As in the private investigator?"

"Mm-hmm." I'm still studying the photograph, trying to understand how we can use this to our advantage.

"But I thought you fired him. June said—"

"I didn't," I interrupt him. "You told me to, but I wanted to see what he could find for us. I'm sorry I didn't tell you. But it doesn't really matter now, does it? This is the first I've heard from him, and it amounts to nothing."

I drop my phone on the nightstand with frustration. At exactly the same time, it chimes again.

I hesitate, but when I pick it up, I see it's another message from Mike. This time, he's sent a link.

I check over my shoulder, where Hudson is watching me. He looks down at the screen, squinting to read it from where he sits.

"What's that?"

"I'm not sure. Only one way to find out." I click on the link, holding my breath as I try to make sense of what he's telling us. When the screen fully loads and I take in what I'm seeing, I gasp.

Hudson leans down closer, his breath hot on my cheek as he struggles to see what I'm looking at. I pass him my phone so he can get a better look, his fingers pinching and zooming as he reads carefully.

"Is this real?"

I nod. "I think so."

"But we didn't find this when we searched for her."

"Mike said something before about having search results scrubbed from the internet. He said he had other ways to find them, though. I guess... I guess this is it."

Another link comes in, interrupting us, and he clicks on it in an instant, holding the phone out so we can both see the website that loads.

My heart pounds, my skin suddenly icy.

Every hair on my body seems to stand on end.

"What the..." Hudson whispers, lifting the phone closer to his nose.

Is it possible?

"Oh my god," he whispers.

When I look at my husband, his eyes are filled with an unreadable expression. "Oh. My. God."

# CHAPTER THIRTY-ONE

## HUDSON

We wait for dark.

Like Maddie's phone calls and the jobs I've taken that have saved us at times and ruined us at others, we wait for the first signs of dusk to settle in.

We've spent the entire afternoon and evening forming a plan with practically every contingency covered. Just hours ago, we were sure this was over, but by a small twist of fate, we seem to have been thrown a lifeline and we are hanging on with both hands.

When darkness falls and the last hint of light disappears from outside our windows, we know it's time. We should be exhausted from a lack of proper sleep and nutrition this weekend, or terrified of how this may all go wrong, but I feel oddly exhilarated. Delirious from hope and happiness and possibility. If we can pull this off, there's a chance we'll make it through unscathed.

We shower together, kissing under the steady stream

of water like honeymooners. It's as if we've been given a second chance at everything.

A chance to start over without any secrets. With everything laid out in front of us. With our worst fears realized and conquered.

We dress in silence, focusing on the task at hand. In my head, I'm running through the plan again. This will work, won't it? We can't fail.

It's almost time.

Willa grabs her keys from the bowl by the door and tosses mine to me. We slip on our jackets, and I try to hide the way my hands are shaking. We've decided to drive separately, just in case something goes wrong, but we're heading to the same place.

Before we leave, I kiss her one more time. I refuse to think of it as the last time.

"We're going to be okay," I say, maybe for her benefit as much as mine. I need it to be true. It has to be true.

In the car, I dial June's number.

She answers on the third ring.

"June Cromwell."

"We have a baby."

"Excuse me?" Even through the bitterness, I hear the excitement.

"One of Willa's clients just went into labor and she hasn't chosen an adoptive family. We found you a baby, June."

"When? When can I get it? Is it a boy? Healthy?"

"It's a boy. Healthy, as far as we can tell. We need

you to meet us at my office now. I realize it's late, but it's—"

"I'm on my way."

The call ends, and step one is complete. Despite how much she's hurt us, I can't help feeling guilty for what we're about to do. I can't dwell on it, though.

She's given us no choice.

---

We arrive at the office, and I slip my white coat over my scrubs. We need everything to look the part. When June arrives, I meet her at the door.

The first problem arises when her driver tries to come inside with her. I put a hand up to stop him in his tracks.

"Sorry, just June for now."

She's practically buzzing with excitement, though the man seems skeptical.

"I go where she goes," he grunts.

"I'm afraid that's not possible. We just need her to fill out some paperwork. Only the adoptive parent is allowed in the room. It's a small office and we have safety procedures to follow, especially after hours like this. You'll be able to accompany her into the hospital, but right now, we just need her."

He checks in with her, and they seem to have a silent conversation with me standing between them.

"Of course," I add, "if you don't feel comfortable with that, you can always come back tomorrow and we can see if my boss will make an exception to who can be in the room. As I'm sure you know, skin-to-skin contact in the first hour of an infant's life is very important for bonding between baby and mother. I'd hoped to be able to get you in the room for that tonight, but if you can't make it work, we'll have to have the birth mother do it instead."

What I'm saying isn't fair or true, but she's high on a nearly reached dream and doesn't seem to care. She gives a flick of her wrist, dismissing the man. "Oh, just wait in the car, will you?"

Reluctantly, he does as she's told him to.

Crisis number one averted.

When I open the door and lead her down the long hallway and then to my office, she freezes at seeing Willa waiting behind my desk.

"What is this? Where is my baby?"

"He's coming," Willa says.

"Paperwork, remember?" I remind her of the conversation we had three seconds ago. "Focus, June. I know you're excited, but we have to discuss a few things with you first."

"What things?" June demands, not budging.

I place a hand on her back, nudging her toward the chair in front of my desk. "Come on, sit. It's a happy day. Let's get the paperwork out of the way so you can go to the hospital."

She seems unsure but eventually sits down, resting her handbag on her lap.

"Is he here yet? Is she still in labor?"

"He's not here just yet. Soon, though. How are you feeling?" I ask.

"I'm feeling like we should get on with this," June snips.

I walk around behind my wife, pulling the manila folder we've prepared out of my drawer. "Let's get on with it, then, shall we?"

I drop it in front of my wife. Willa rests her hands on top of the folder. I know she's struggling with this, with the guilt of everything she's done and everything we're doing, but even with that hesitation, she's such a natural at this. I can't help being in awe of her calmness. Her surety. She's so still. So patient.

"So, you see, June, when I start a new client file, I have to do all the usual checks. Background, sex offender registry, credit, and so on and so forth." She bends the corner of the folder mindlessly, rolling it between her fingers. "I really want to dig into the lives of my adoptive parents to make sure we're placing these babies in loving and fit homes."

"What are you saying?" June asks, looking between us.

"Well, obviously, because this wasn't a classic case, I may have skipped a few steps in the beginning. I didn't look into you enough. I didn't look further than your old application, in fact. Then again, you did have us quite frazzled, so I hope you'll forgive that little oversight." She pats the folder. "But I've more than made up for it now."

June's eyes narrow. "What are you talking about?"

"Well, you want to be sure we place babies in safe

homes, don't you? Surely you wouldn't want an infant in the home of a criminal."

"The only criminals in this room are you." June grips the handles of her purse, moving to stand.

"Well…" Willa carries out the word, looking up at me. "I'm afraid that's not entirely true, and you know it." She opens the folder and slides it across the desk.

June sits back down and leans forward, staring at the photograph sent to us by the private investigator. She trails a pointed, black fingernail along the outline of her body in the picture.

"What the hell is this? What are you implying? It's not a crime to kiss someone in public."

"No, no, you're right. Maybe kissing someone in public isn't illegal, or even wrong necessarily." I put a hand on my wife's shoulder. "But I think we can all agree necrophilia is frowned upon." The air is sucked from the room, tension palpable, as the implication in my words hangs on the silence. Her eyes lift to meet mine, and the sharpness there is cutting.

"What the hell are you talking about?"

"You know what they say, June. Those who live in glass houses"—Willa lifts the photograph, sliding it out of the way to reveal the next page—"*shouldn't throw stones.*"

June stares at the paper—at the article sent to us by the private investigator—in enraged horror. Though I'd been inclined to underestimate Mike, he'd turned out to be worth his weight in gold.

I nudge the page forward, letting her get a good look

at the article detailing her husband's extensive list of mostly white-collar crimes.

"Tax evasion, wire fraud, bookkeeping fraud, extortion. You really learned that one from the best, didn't you?" I lean down over the desk, tapping the paper.

June rips the folder out from under my finger, her lips moving as she reads the words. She eyes the photo again. "Where did you get these?"

"There are more of them. We made copies, obviously."

"I paid to have them hidden," she says. "No one was supposed to be able to find them."

I shrug. "Better get a refund, then."

Her eyes narrow. "You have no idea who you're messing with, Mr. Ashley."

"It's *Dr.* Ashley," I correct her, "and yes, I think we do know." I jab my finger into the paper again. "We've spent a lot of time reading, June. A lot of time learning. We have you all figured out."

"You do?" she challenges, standing up so we're practically nose to nose.

"We do." I don't budge.

"Enlighten me."

"Your husband commits all these crimes, gets caught, and then, days before he's charged and arrested, he dies. That would ordinarily be a very tragic story, if he wasn't still *driving you around.*"

She shoves her hands down at her sides in contempt. "You are messing with the wrong people. You think this has been bad? You have no idea what I can do. How miserable I can make your life, do you hear me?"

"Oh, we hear you loud and clear, but you see, you don't have any leverage against us anymore. We're fully prepared to go to the police. In fact, before we discovered this, we were ready to walk into a station and confess everything, but then, this all sort of fell into our laps." I gesture toward the article still gripped in her fist. "And we thought we'd offer you one final out."

She drops the paper onto the desk and reaches into her purse. I spot her hand land on a gun I hadn't noticed earlier. My stomach clenches. "I wouldn't do that if I were you."

She meets my eyes with a challenge, but doesn't immediately pull it out. "Why's that?"

"We just got our security upgraded. New cameras." I point to the two cameras in both corners of my office. "You walked by half a dozen more on your way in. Each one will have captured your face on it. The footage is stored off-site and uploaded to the cloud. I've already told my boss I had to come in to work late tonight. Which means if anything happens to us, the first thing they'll do is pull the footage. And they'll see you, June. There's no way around that. If you kill us right now, you will go down for murder."

She looks down, then back up, heaving a heavy breath. Reluctantly, her hand releases the gun and she places her bag down. Finally, she wraps one arm around herself, the wrinkles around her lips deepening. "Fine.

You said you're offering me a final out. What is it? I'm listening."

I fight against my grin. "Right. Look, the bottom line is everyone in this room has done some bad things. We can all agree on that. But whose crime is the worst? I'm willing to go down for what I did. Willa, too. If that's what you need."

Willa lifts our phones in the air, tapping each of the screens. "We are not recording you, for the record. This isn't a trap. I know you have proof of what I did, and that's fine. If you want to turn me in, be my guest. Hudson, too. But know now that, if you do, we will tell them that your husband is alive and well and driving Miss Daisy all around town."

"And I realize now that he was the man in the room with you the day you framed me. It was never another escort. You guys did this together. All of it. So, we'd be telling them that, too," I add.

I'm making an educated guess, but June's silence is enough confirmation. It was the two of them all along.

"But there is another choice," Willa says, cutting through the silence. Her voice is softer. Hopeful. "Something that will work for all of us."

June's chin quivers, and she wavers. Her hands lift up to her sides powerlessly. "Not for me. Don't you get that? This is it. This *was* it. The only way to fix anything."

"I don't believe that, June," Willa says.

"Frankly, Willa, I don't give a damn what you think." June's eyes whip up to meet hers, then mine. "You both think you've got it all figured out, don't you?" Her lips upturn into a small, sad smile. "You think you're so smart and you've just put this little problem to rest. Well, let me be the first to break the news to you. You still don't know the truth about what's happening. You still"—she pauses as if she's realizing it right as the words leave her mouth— "even after all this time, have no idea why you're here."

# CHAPTER THIRTY-TWO

## WILLA

"What does that mean?" I ask. "Why do you think we're here?"

June sits down in the chair, tossing one leg over the other. She runs a hand through her hair.

"You know, my son wasn't even supposed to be at that party." Her voice is sharp. Accusatory. "He was nineteen. Too old for high school parties. It was his friend, Connor, that dragged him along. The police never confirmed it, but a mother always knows."

She wrings her shaking hands together, looking everywhere but at us. "After Nathan died, my world imploded. My marriage. David started working more. At least, that's what he called it." She rolls her eyes. "I think he just looked for any excuse to be away from me, truth be told."

The honesty in her words stings me, but I can't let myself forget what she's done. Still, knowing I caused this pain, not just for her but for eight other families, it would be enough to take me under if I let it.

"I don't know if that's when everything started to get out of control, but that's when I started noticing things weren't quite right. The missing money. The whispered phone calls. I was too wrapped up in my loss to care. I looked the other way for so long it became a practice in our house. He left the house, I didn't ask where he was going. He said we didn't have the money for something, I didn't ask why. He brought new friends over, I didn't ask where they'd met. While I lost myself in grief over what we'd lost, my husband lost himself in work trying to build something new."

She isn't crying, even as she talks about what must've been the worst time of her life, but there's a stoic, quiet sense of pain there that cuts deep.

"By the time I caught on, it was too late. He'd slipped up on some loan document, gotten the attention of the wrong people. When he told me, it was like he was saying goodbye. Even as he promised we'd fight it, I could see that he knew it was a lost cause."

She swipes a finger under her eye, though I still don't see any tears, and brushes her hair back from her face. "Well, I couldn't lose someone else. Simple as that. Not after what I'd been through. I refused to lose him. So, we made a plan. Er, well, I made a plan. He had to die. It was the only way. He was supposed to leave the country after it happened. I was going to join him after the investigation was closed—once things settled down. I had to have the funeral first. Look the part. Play the grieving widow."

She purses her lips, nodding. Confirming to herself, it seems, that it was still the right plan. "As much as I wanted to, I couldn't go with him, not right away. It would look too suspicious. But, when the time came for him to go, he just... He didn't. Couldn't, he said. He couldn't leave me. At the time, his staying felt like the most selfless thing he'd ever done for me. He didn't want me to be alone, truly alone, for the first time since I was twenty-nine years old."

She clears her throat, looking away. "Of course, that was before I knew about the affairs."

I swallow. "Affairs?"

"Yes." She nods as if we should've pieced it together by then. "One of the women was your friend. Murphy Masters. Believe it or not, *she*, not you, Willa, is the reason for all of this."

"What?" I shake my head, trying to understand. "No. That doesn't make any sense."

"The married man," Hudson says, his voice heavy with the weight of what we're learning. "In Murphy's therapy tape. She was talking about your husband?"

"Yes," June confirms. "She'd been sleeping with David for quite some time. To be honest, I don't know how long. I can't get a straight answer from him, even now. He's ten years younger than I am—maybe that should've been a reason to stay away back then—but I was utterly in awe of him right from the start. We fell for each other hard and fast, and we were married six months later. A few years after that, Nathan was born and our family was complete."

"I'm sorry, I'm still trying to understand. You're saying your husband is sleeping with Murphy?" I ask.

"Yes." The answer is matter of fact and emotionless. "Even after his *death*"—she raises her brows at the word—"the affair didn't stop. She was just one of many for him, even after he'd gotten her pregnant. There was no attachment on his part, but I was determined to put an end to it, like the others. Most of the women were only with him for his money, or at least that was a huge part of it, so I'd been able to pay them off. A few I scared off when the money wasn't enough, but Murphy wasn't so easy. She was resilient. I might admire that quality if it didn't piss me off so badly."

"How did you get the tape? The recording?" My own voice sounds foreign to me. I'm breathless, my head fuzzy with newfound revelations.

"I had her followed and found out she was in therapy. Then I just paid her therapist to send me recordings of their sessions," she says. "It wasn't hard. Especially since the therapist she chose was sleeping with at least two of his clients."

"That's terrible." I don't mean for the words to sneak out, but they do under my breath. I look up at her with a cold stare, fury pulsing in my veins. "She trusted him and he betrayed her. She was in therapy to get better. How could you do this?"

June pauses. "She was sleeping with my husband. What would you do?"

*Everything.*

The answer is there, in the quiet part of my brain.

When I don't answer, she goes on, "At first, the sessions were about her pregnancy, but when she started talking about her past, she mentioned something that caught my attention. Something I cared more about than where my husband chooses to spend his nights."

"The fire. That's how you knew about the fire." It all clicks into place for me, finally. All the missing pieces.

"Yes. She told the therapist about a fire she'd been involved in around a decade ago. A party where people got hurt. She didn't go into details, exactly. Nothing incriminating or specific. Little details were mixed up, I'm assuming purposefully. But she mentioned that there was a fire she felt responsible for. That she'd never told anyone she was there with her best friend. That they'd both done something terrible that night." She narrows her eyes at me. "So, of course, I had to find this best friend, and lo and behold, here you are."

"So, let me get this straight, Murphy is sleeping with your husband, she's having his child, and she was involved in the fire that killed your son, and yet, you came after *us*? Why?" Hudson asks.

I hate the question, but I can't deny how badly I want to know the answer.

"Well, *you*"—her eyes dart to Hudson—"you just happened to be collateral damage with a job I could easily take advantage of." When she looks back at me, there is no apology waiting. "*You*, on the other hand, were a much more appropriate target than Murphy. That girl's life is a mess. She's broke, sleeping with men who don't care about her. She has no ambition, no house, no life. You were there that night too, equally guilty based on what she'd said, and yet, here you sit, living a perfect little life after you robbed my son of his."

I take a measured breath, letting it out slowly to keep calm. She wants to get a rise out of me, but I refuse to give in. "I did not kill your son, June. I was there, yes. I knew about the fire and I tried to warn everyone. But I had to get myself out, too. I was sixteen years old. Just a kid myself. That doesn't excuse it. I'm not saying I don't bear some guilt, because of course I do, but I am not a trained firefighter. I couldn't drag people out. No one would listen until it was too late."

"Did you call the police?"

It's the one question that will always stop me in my tracks, the question that will forever put an end to any moment when I'm feeling proud of myself. Any moment that doesn't feel a bit like self-loathing. The question that will silence any voice inside of me that says I did all I could.

It's always there—despite what I tell Hudson, despite what I tell Murphy, despite what I tell myself half the time. The guilt gnaws at me. It festers. It won't leave, and maybe it shouldn't. Maybe that's the cross I bear for what I did.

But I am not a murderer. I need her to know that. I need her to know that I tried. That I would've given anything to make sure her son came home to her that night.

As if expecting me not to answer, June goes on, "You,

my dear, were bigger fish to fry. You were happy. You'd moved on. Nathan was never afforded such a luxury."

"I haven't moved on. Not by a long shot. That night still haunts me. How could it not? Maybe from the outside, it does look like I'm doing okay, but it's all an act. I'm hurting. I'll always hurt over what happened. It's as much a part of me as my hair or my skin. But I try to do right in every way I can. I try to help. To be a good person. It's all I can do."

"It's not enough," she says calmly. "It will never be enough."

"I'm sorry, June, truly I am, but that's not for you to decide." I say the words as gently as possible. "I can give you my apology and the truth of what happened that night, but your forgiveness is something I have to be okay living without."

"So, okay, you found Murphy," Hudson prompts, distracting June from the malice in her stare, "you listened to her sessions and discovered what happened that night, and then what? Made a plan? This plan?"

"Yes. It was simple, really. It *should* have been simple. Once I'd located Willa, I had you both followed. I saw you with Constance, Hudson, realized what you are, and the plan began to take shape." Her eyes cut to me. "I will never get my Nathan back, but the least you can do is give me a child to replace the one you stole from me." For the first time, her voice cracks when she says, "I was a good mother. When David was supposed to leave, I tried to find a baby to adopt. I didn't want to be alone, but nothing I said or did mattered. No one would help me.

The agencies all turned me down. I'd almost given up when I found Murphy. And she led me to you. I have to believe that's fate. You were meant to help me."

I lay my hands out flat in front of me, bouncing them in the air slowly. "I can't give you a baby, June. I'm sorry. I can't. And if that means you're going to turn me in, knowing the consequences, so be it. If you'd like to try to kill us, I guess you'll have to try. But, what I will do is let you go. I will offer you that grace because I do understand why you did this. If you walk out of this room right now, I will never tell a soul about your husband." I gesture toward Hudson. "*We* will never tell a soul. I'm so sorry that Nathan was taken from you, but *I* didn't take him. You still have a life. You still have a husband, if that's what you want. Take him and go. Leave the country like you'd planned. Live your life. Like Nathan would've wanted. None of this has to end any worse than it already is."

"He cheated," she says, looking away. I catch a glint of a tear in her eye. "He lied to me. How can I ever move on from that?"

I'm quiet for a moment, thinking. "Maybe you can't," I say eventually. Softly. "But a baby won't fix that. Only you can fix it. Only you know how."

She sniffles, rubbing a hand under her nose. "I could kill you, you know. I have the means. With one phone call, you could be dead."

"We know." Hudson grabs my hands. "But we don't think you will. Killing us doesn't get you anything you want."

"It protects our secret."

"You're wrong about that. We've already said we'll protect yours as long as you protect ours," he says. "You have our word. But, if you do kill us, we have made arrangements to release your secret upon our deaths. A letter will be delivered to our lawyer detailing everything we know."

Her eyes bounce back and forth between us, her mouth opening once, then closing. Finally, without another word, June dries her eyes and stands up, shoulders back. You'd never have known we just saw her break, if only for a second.

I watch her cross the room. She pauses at the door and looks back for just a second. "There was... There was never really a baby, was there?"

I press my lips together with an apologetic frown, an answer given.

"Right." She nods, pulls open the door, and disappears through it without another word.

Hudson lowers himself down beside me. "We did it." He pulls me into a hug, kissing my cheek. I breathe him in. "It actually worked. That was brilliant. *You* were brilliant."

I lean farther into his embrace, though I can't seem to muster the sort of enthusiasm he has. "We're not out of the woods yet."

"Did you see her, though? She's not going to tell. There'd be no point. We thought of everything. She can't deny that we're right. There's nothing left to be done except move on. For all of us."

I nod. It does feel over. We won, whatever that's worth. Still, I don't feel like celebrating. June isn't a monster I take pride in defeating because I don't think she is truly a monster at all.

She's just a brokenhearted mother, like so many of the clients I see coming through my office.

Either way, Hudson's right. The only thing left to do is move on. I have to believe I'm capable of that. With everything out on the table, maybe now we can all finally heal.

That's what truth does, doesn't it?

Heals. Sets you free.

It's all I've ever wanted, after all.

I guess, in a strange way, I have June to thank for that.

# CHAPTER THIRTY-THREE

## WILLA

## SIX MONTHS LATER

"Alright. That's everything." The movers slam the back of the truck shut after the last of the moving boxes are loaded inside.

As we stand outside our house for the last time, Hudson wraps an arm around my waist, drawing me into his side.

"Are you going to miss this place?"

"Maybe a little," I admit.

It's true, really. In some ways, I know there are things that I'll miss. This house is full of amazing memories. It's the first house we owned together. The first kitchen we renovated. Five years of birthday cakes and anniversary meals were baked under this roof. There was the celebratory dinner we had when Hudson got hired out of residency. The love we shared within these walls will always be a part of me. But there are memories I'd rather forget here, too. Memories I'd rather outrun. To move on, we have to leave this place behind.

Finally, I feel ready.

"Ready to roll?" one of the movers asks, practically reading my mind as he walks by, jingling the keys in his hand.

"Yeah, we're ready to head out," Hudson says. "Just gotta lock up."

The man nods and joins the rest of the crew as they climb into the front of the moving van. Hudson makes his way to the front door to lock it. He picks up the welcome mat we carefully chose last fall.

To my left, the sound of a baby's cry draws my attention. I spin around to face them, my face lighting up in an instant smile.

Finally, I see the appeal of babies. Families.

Murphy appears from beside her car. Her hair is cut shorter now, so Aiden can't grab it, though he still tries his hardest. She holds her son in her arms with the confidence and sense of calm of someone who's been doing it for years.

Despite her hesitations and a few road bumps along the way, being a mother seems to have come naturally to my best friend.

"Have we got everything?" she asks, bouncing him gently to soothe his cries.

"That's the last of it." I eye her car, loaded down with boxes. "What about you? Did you get the rest of what was left at your apartment?"

"Yeah, I loaded the last few things while he slept. It wasn't much."

"You're not going to know what to do with all your new space," I tell her. And it's true. The new house we've bought has enough space for all of us to live together, for Aiden to have a yard to play in, for family dinners and huge Christmases none of us ever had. It has space for love and growth and a lifetime of happiness.

I think through all of this, the thing I've learned is that family is what you make it. None of us came from perfect families—there are things we all want to change— but we don't have to do it alone.

Our family has grown in unexpected ways because of what happened. There are no more secrets, no more lies. Everything is out in the open, and we're better for it.

Though I hate to admit it, June saved us as much as she hurt us. I think I'll always feel indebted to her for that.

As we make our way to the car, I rub a finger over my godson's cloud-soft hand. His fingers open on instinct, reaching for me. He feels so safe, his eyes never even open. He knows we have him. That he's loved. Protected.

Murphy's eyes fill with tears, as if she can sense my thoughts.

"Luckiest kid ever," she whispers.

"Best kid ever," I add.

I help her load Aiden into his car seat and then give her the new house key. It's been placed onto a key chain with the realtor's logo. "Hudson is going to stop by the realtor's office to turn in the keys, so I'm giving this to you because you'll beat us both there. That's the only one for now, so don't lose it. We'll have to make copies once we get there."

She hesitates. "Are you sure you want to give it to me?"

"Yes, I'm sure. I trust you." I bump her hip with mine.

"Where will you be?"

"I'll be there. I just have to make a quick pit stop. Oh. *Shoot.* I didn't think about it, but do you want Hudson to ride with you to help keep him calm? We can always leave his car at the realtor's office and come back for it if you want to follow him over there."

"Thanks, but I've got this. He sleeps pretty well in the car, and I just fed him, so he should be okay for a while."

"Okay, cool. Just meet the movers at the house, then, and show them where everything goes, please."

"Okay. Will do. You guys be careful."

"Yeah, you too."

I wave at her as she slides into the driver's seat.

Hudson jogs past me and opens the passenger door, leaning down to see her. "Careful at the state line. Cops'll be bad. And be sure to let the movers know which rooms are which."

"Will do." She salutes us playfully and starts the car. As she backs away, following the movers, Hudson turns to me, holding out his hand.

"Are you ready to go?"

I take it. "As I'll ever be."

Twenty minutes across town doesn't compare to the six-hour drive we have ahead of us to our new home, but still, it feels unending.

When I pull up in front of the gated estate, I roll the window down and press a button to call the house.

Within minutes, I hear June's voice. "Yes?"

Until this moment, I wasn't sure if she'd have left as we suggested. To be honest, I'm not sure if I was hoping she'd be gone.

"It's... It's me, June. Can I come in?"

My request is met by silence, and I half expect her to ignore me or refuse to open the gate. We haven't spoken since that day at Hudson's old office. I wouldn't blame her if she didn't want to see me.

To my surprise, within seconds, the gate swings open, allowing me to drive through. Up close, the house is even more stunning than I imagined. The stark-white stone shines in the sunlight, its columns grand and proud.

As I get closer, I realize June is standing on the terrace, watching me drive up. I park the car and open the door slowly. When I get out of the car, she moves closer. She's obviously uneasy, as am I.

"Hi." I round the car.

Her eyes drift to the paper in my hand and then, almost as if she's afraid to ask, she says, "He was born, wasn't he? The baby? I've been watching the birth announcements in the paper, but... I thought, well, I worried something may have gone wrong."

There won't have been any announcement, at Murphy's insistence that no one reads the newspapers anymore anyway, but I don't need to tell her that.

Instead, I hold out the photograph I've printed for her. The one of Aiden's tiny, pink body swaddled in a white cloth at the hospital on the day he was born.

"Nothing went wrong," I assure her.

She takes it with delicate fingers, like she's afraid it might crumble from being touched. Tears fill her blue eyes instantly.

"Oh." One hand goes to her mouth. Her usual stony face is transformed by pure joy, the wrinkles around her eyes deepening as she bends at the waist, taking in the sight of him. "Oh my. Oh, sweet boy. Is he... He looks healthy. Is he healthy?"

"Perfectly healthy."

"Of course he is. He has good blood." She traces a finger across his nose, then his bottom lip. "And he was... Was he a good size? Not too little? He looks so little. It's hard to believe they're ever that little."

"He was perfect. Seven pounds, nine ounces. Twenty inches long."

She smiles at the photograph, her chin quivering as her finger moves to caress his forehead. "He... He has his eyes. He has Nathan's eyes."

She says the words so softly I almost don't hear them, and when she looks up at me, it's all I can do to hold it together.

"Thank you." She takes my hand, squeezing it. "Can

I... I mean, I don't suppose I could see him? Just for a few minutes?"

"No," I say, looking away. "I'm sorry, but it's not possible. He's already been adopted. He will be living with a family out of state." It's the one lie I will tell her. A lie necessary to protect Murphy and Aiden. "But he is so loved, June. I wanted you to know that. He is so, so loved."

She nods. "Did you meet them? Are they good people?"

"They're great people. I couldn't have picked them better myself. I promise you he will have an amazing life."

"You didn't have to do this, you know?" she says, studying my face in a way that tells me she wants to ask why I did, but she doesn't dare.

"I wanted you to know he exists. It felt important. I wanted you to know that he's healthy and happy and cared for."

She dries her tears, fanning her eyes, and steps back. "Well, I suppose it's for the best, isn't it?" She starts to pass the photograph back to me, but I hold up a hand.

"No. It's for you to keep."

She clutches it to her chest like a lifeline. She doesn't need to say thank you again. It's written all over her face.

"Take care of yourself, June," I tell her.

A wish.

A prayer.

A hope.

She nods and glances up toward the front door.

"Always do. I'm, uh, selling the house, you know. It's a... It's a big house. Too big for just one person."

Relief at what she's telling me swallows me up. I smile softly. Just enough. "Yes. I suppose it is."

Without another word, I walk back around the car and slide into my seat. I don't have to look back at her as she makes her way toward the house to know she's still studying the photograph, looking for any hints of the son she lost.

I wonder if she'll show the photograph to David at some point, though something tells me he'd never care as much as she seems to. To my knowledge, he's not reached out to Murphy a single time since Aiden's birth.

Not that she needs him.

Once we showed her the article about his crimes, let her know how dangerous he is, she was finally able to walk away. To know that she deserves better.

That Aiden deserves better.

She's going to be alright.

We all are.

I check the rearview once more as I pull away, knowing this will be the last time I see June Cromwell. The last time I see this town, most likely.

Somewhere, less than an hour ahead of me, I have a sweet, amazing man on his way to our new home. When I arrive, he'll be waiting for me. Waiting for me to slip my hand into his and get ready to build a new life together in a place neither of us has any history.

A place where June will never find us.

Where we can move on from our past and look toward the future.

A safe place.

A place where our godson will live without fear, without worrying where his next meal will come from or whether he still has a roof over his head and a warm place to sleep.

A life where his family will consist of his godparents and his mother, and who knows, maybe someday a dog. I'm still not set on kids of my own, but we haven't ruled it out. Aiden is growing on me, that's for certain.

Together, we've created a life better than the three of us could've ever imagined. Whatever the future holds, I know we'll be together. That we'll be okay.

June gave us that.

I thought we'd had a great marriage before. Truly, I did. We were happy and I loved him, but whatever we had then was nothing compared to now. We've gone through so much together in such a short period of time, and it's done everything to make us stronger.

I guess that's how it works, in a way.

Sometimes, even when you feel like your relationship is strong, even when you think you're destined to be together forever, you have to wait for the dark times to come along to prove your strength. Darkness will always find us. There's no escaping it. No outrunning it. We have to be ready to fight our way through it, no matter the cost.

Hudson and I learned that the hard way.

But if you can wait for the dark, if you can hold out

and survive the darkness, and if you can forge your path through whatever comes your way together, it only goes on to show you how bright the light can be.

When you've been to hell and back like we have, when your love is rooted in friendship and kindness and grace, there's no longer a question of what you can do together.

What you'll be willing to do *for* each other.

I guess it's funny, really. Hudson and I both worked for lives where we could build families for other people. Create something from nothing. Add love where it wasn't before. We wanted to give people the lives we never had.

I just never imagined the family we'd be most proud of building would be our own.

## DON'T MISS THE NEXT PSYCHOLOGICAL THRILLER FROM KIERSTEN MODGLIN!

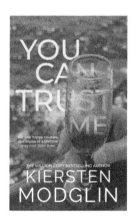

For two happy couples, the cruise
of a lifetime may cost their lives.

Purchase *You Can Trust Me* today:
https://mybook.to/youcantrustme

## WOULD YOU RECOMMEND WAIT FOR DARK?

If you enjoyed this story, please consider leaving me a quick review. It doesn't have to be long—just a few words will do. Who knows? Your review might be the thing that encourages a future reader to take a chance on my work!

To leave a review, please visit:

https://mybook.to/waitfordark

Let everyone know how much you loved
*Wait for Dark* on Goodreads:
https://bit.ly/waitfordarkthriller

## STAY UP TO DATE ON EVERYTHING KMOD!

Thank you so much for reading this story. I'd love to invite you to sign up for my mailing list and text alerts so we can be sure you don't miss my next release.

Sign up for my mailing list here:
kierstenmodglinauthor.com/nlsignup

Sign up for my text alerts here:
kierstenmodglinauthor.com/textalerts

# ACKNOWLEDGMENTS

As always, I should start by thanking my amazing husband and sweet little girl—thank you for letting me chase my dream and for being here every step of the way. I love you both so very much.

To my wonderful editor, Sarah West—thank you for helping my stories shine, for always trusting my instincts, and for your incredible advice and insight. You're the best!

To the awesome proofreading team at My Brother's Editor, Rosa and Ellie—thank you for being my final set of eyes! I'm so grateful for you guys!

To my loyal readers (AKA the #KMod Squad)—thank you for being excited for each new book, for cheering me on, for leaving amazing reviews, for every single email, social media tag, recommendation to friends and family, book club call, and shout out. I still feel the need to pinch myself over what a dream come true you all are. I'm so thankful for each of you!

To my book club/gang/besties—Sara, both Erins, June, Heather, and Dee—thank you for being a highlight of my week, for always making me laugh, for the vent sessions, the laughter, the tears, and the friendship. Love you, girls.

To my bestie, Emerald O'Brien—thank you for everything. My gosh, where do I even start?! Thank you for being the first one to hear my story ideas and never getting tired of talking through plot problems and character issues. Thank you for doing life with me, through every stage of this crazy career. I love you. Same moon.

To Becca and Lexy—thank you for keeping me on track, for all the memes, and for making me look like I know what I'm doing.

To June Costello—thank you for loving Coralee from *The Mother-in-Law* so much that when I started writing this character who reminded me so much of her, I knew she could only be named after you. I'm so grateful for your support and friendship. I hope you love your wild, headstrong namesake.

Last but certainly not least, to you, dear reader—thank you for purchasing this book and supporting my dream. When I write my stories, I'm always thinking about the person on the other side of this book. I wonder which parts will shock you, which characters you'll root for, and what storylines will resonate with you. I hope that this book kept you entertained and guessing every step of the way. And, as always, whether this was your first Kiersten Modglin book or your 38th, I hope it was everything you hoped for and nothing like you expected.

# ABOUT THE AUTHOR

KIERSTEN MODGLIN is an Amazon Top 10 bestselling author of psychological thrillers. Her books have sold over a million copies and been translated into multiple languages. Kiersten is a member of International Thriller Writers, Novelists, Inc., and the Alliance of Independent Authors. She is a KDP Select All-Star and a recipient of *ThrillerFix*'s Best Psychological Thriller Award, *Suspense Magazine*'s Best Book of 2021 Award, a 2022 Silver Falchion for Best Suspense, and a 2022 Silver Falchion for Best Overall Book of 2021. Kiersten grew up in rural western Kentucky and later relocated to Nashville, Tennessee, where she now lives with her family. Kiersten's readers across the world lovingly refer to her as "KMod." A binge-watching expert, psychology fanatic, and *indoor* enthusiast, Kiersten enjoys rainy days spent with her favorite people and evenings with her nose in a book.

Sign up for Kiersten's newsletter here:
kierstenmodglinauthor.com/nlsignup

Sign up for text alerts from Kiersten here:
kierstenmodglinauthor.com/textalerts

kierstenmodglinauthor.com
www.facebook.com/kierstenmodglinauthor
www.facebook.com/groups/kmodsquad
www.twitter.com/kmodglinauthor
www.instagram.com/kierstenmodglinauthor
www.tiktok.com/@kierstenmodglinauthor
www.goodreads.com/kierstenmodglinauthor
www.bookbub.com/authors/kiersten-modglin
www.amazon.com/author/kierstenmodglin

ALSO BY KIERSTEN MODGLIN

**<u>STANDALONE NOVELS</u>**

Becoming Mrs. Abbott

The List

The Missing Piece

Playing Jenna

The Beginning After

The Better Choice

The Good Neighbors

The Lucky Ones

I Said Yes

The Mother-in-Law

The Dream Job

The Nanny's Secret

The Liar's Wife

My Husband's Secret

The Perfect Getaway

The Roommate

The Missing

Just Married

Our Little Secret

Widow Falls

Missing Daughter

The Reunion

Tell Me the Truth

The Dinner Guests

If You're Reading This...

A Quiet Retreat

The Family Secret

Don't Go Down There

You Can Trust Me

## ARRANGEMENT TRILOGY

The Arrangement (Book 1)

The Amendment (Book 2)

The Atonement (Book 3)

## THE MESSES SERIES

The Cleaner (Book 1)

The Healer (Book 2)

The Liar (Book 3)

The Prisoner (Book 4)

## NOVELLAS

The Long Route: A Lover's Landing Novella

The Stranger in the Woods: A Crimson Falls Novella

Made in United States
North Haven, CT
06 May 2024

52163101R00157